THUNDER TIME

BOOK 19

CRAIG HALLORAN

Thunder Time: Dragon Wars - Book 19

By Craig Halloran

★★★★★

TWO-TEN BOOK PRESS

PO Box 4215, Charleston, WV 25364

WWW.DRAGONWARSBOOKS.COM

ISBN PAPERBACK: 9798450573816

ISBN HARDBACK: 9781087982892

Publisher's Note

This book is a work of fiction. Names, characters, places, and incidents either are the product of the author's imagination or are used fictitiously, and any resemblance to actual persons, living or dead, events, or locales is entirely coincidental.

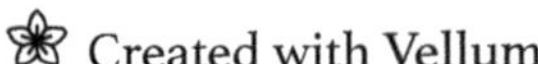 Created with Vellum

Gapoli
ICE VALE
UGRAD
DARK MOUNTAIN
FAR STICK
LOOSE BOOT
CRACK SCOWL
BLACK STOW
KENNA
DAGGER FORD
GREEN RIDGE
AGUSTUN
STAATUS
INLAND SEA
WESTERLUND
MONARCH CITY
ARROW WOOD
DOVERUN
THE GREAT RIVER
DORTAM
HARBOR LAKE
RAVEN CLIFF
THE OUTER RING
NAALUM
FERRY LUNN
IRON HILLS
RED BONE
THE OLD WILLOWACKS
HAVENSTOCK
FARHOOK
SALT KNOB
OLDHAM
MORTUS
SULTER SLAY
DEBBLE BOLT
VALLEY SHIRE
HOTVALE
LAKE FLUGEN
CROW VALLEY
GUNDER ISLAND
DWARF SKULL
THE SHELF
GOLD HOOK
LITTLETON

WIZARD WATCH: SOUTHEAST GAPOLI

WHAT MEMBERS of Talon remained were outside the Wizard Watch, where they'd set up a camp among Cinder's children.

They'd pitched small tents acquired from Littleton and kept a few campfires going. It was early evening, and most of the members prepared food over the small fires while others wandered around camp.

Crane kept everyone entertained with one unbelievable story after another. The paunchy world traveler sat on the bench seat of his wagon, puffing on a long-stem pipe with an easy smile.

Zanna and Gossamer were a part of his audience. Since Zanna had escaped from the Nether Realm, she'd remained outside, waiting for Grey Cloak and the others to return from Nalzambor. It didn't take long for her to become fully acquainted with the other members of Talon.

Reginald the Razor had proved to be a charmer with wit as sharp as his blades. Gorva the orcen natural was every bit as rugged as her father, Hogrim, whom Zanna had known quite well. Shannon, or Beak, as they sometimes called her, was a fine honor guard from Monarch City, as was Tinison, a bushy-haired fighter who was built like a potato and spoke with a loud, somewhat obnoxious voice.

All of them were weary-eyed. They yawned, napped, and groaned when they got up or sat down. They checked one another's wounds, redressed bandages, and did whatever else they needed together.

Zanna enjoyed the warm evening wind on her face and let her hair down. Crane's gentle voice eased the tension in her muscles. She sat with her back against a cart wheel and listened.

"And there he was," Crane said in a hushed voice. He took a few small puffs from his pipe and huffed out a thick smoke ring. The misty ring, hollow at first, took on the shape of an ugly creature. "A bugbear! The biggest one I ever saw." The smoke image faded.

Crane continued, "He wore a necklace made from halfling skulls, and links of steel earrings hung down from his earlobes to his shoulders. And he stank. The most awful smell that still burns my nose and makes my eyes water when I think about it." He smacked his lips, picked up a jug of wine, and drank. "Sorry, but I had to wash the memory of the foul taste out of my mouth."

Razor, who stood nearby with his fists on his hips, asked, "Well, what did you do?"

"I'm getting there." Crane set down the jug. "So there I was, taking a shortcut through the woods, trying to make it in time for a meeting with the Rogues of Rodden in the cottage town of Dimlay, when I was cut off by this massive highwayman." He stretched out his arms. "His notched-up long sword looked like a butter knife in his hairy grip, and slobber dripped from the corners of his mouth when he spoke.

"Give me your sack," Crane said in a throaty imitation of the bugbear's voice.

"My heart raced. I froze. I didn't know what to say, so I stood there, flat-footed, with my mouth hanging open. Right in front of me stood this towering bugbear with long, greasy hair and beady eyes that were burning with fire."

Gorva, who stood near Razor, asked, "What did you do? Pull a dagger and stab him in the belly?"

"No, I didn't have one on me. I was in such a hurry that I forgot my belt and had enough trouble keeping my trousers up," Crane replied. "I walked the entire time with one hand keeping my pants hitched up."

"Enough about the pants," Razor demanded. "What happened?"

Gorva nudged him. "Don't be rude."

"But his stories take forever."

"It's not as if you have anything else to do," Gorva said.

Zanna grinned. After being turned into a statue for many seasons, she enjoyed nothing more than the voices of bickering people again.

By that time, everyone in the small camp had gathered around. Even Cinder's sons and daughters, lounging in the tall grasses, had their heads up and their eyes open.

"So," Crane said, "I finally got some feeling in my extremities, and under the canopy of branches, I took a straight look into the brooding, shadowed face of the bugbear. Something clicked in me—a strange familiarity. I squinted and leaned in."

In his gravelly bugbear voice Crane said, "Come any closer, and I'll plant my sword in your melon head."

"I thought, *Who is he calling a melon head? Isn't that the pot calling the kettle black? His is as big and ugly as a pumpkin patch.*" Crane puffed on his pipe. "Except I didn't actually think it. I said it out loud. And with a straight face."

Razor groaned. "What happened?"

"I'm getting there. You see, the prickliness of the atmosphere faded, and the bugbear tilted his melon head to one side. Then he said one word to me that I'll never forget." He paused.

All eyes in the camp were fastened on him.

He blew out a long stream of smoke and said, "'Crane?'"

"'Overt? Is that you?' I asked."

"'It's me. Overt!' He stepped into a spot of moonlight bleeding through the branches, and I got my first clear look at his ugly face. This time, my pounding heart was full of glee when Overt put away his sword and offered his hand.'"

"Then did you stab him?" Razor interjected.

"What? No. Overt and I were old friends, from decades back. He escorted me all the way back to Dimlay, where I set him up with the Rogues of Rodden."

"Ah, that story's awful," Slicer said. He had moseyed in behind Reginald and Gorva. "I'm with Razor. I'd have gutted the bugbear the moment he exposed himself and eaten him for dinner."

Crane grinned. "You would never have gotten past the smell."

"Speaking of smells..." Gorva's nostrils flared. "Someone let the stinky cheese out."

"Wasn't me," Razor said as he pinched his nose. "Ew!"

The foul smell spread, and everyone, man and dragon, covered their noses.

"Zooks!" someone stated. "Is this the kind of welcome heroes should expect when they return home? We should have stayed in Nalzambor."

Zanna rose. Her heart swelled when she laid eyes on her son, Dyphestive, Zora, Anya, and Streak.

Crane shouted, "Grey Cloak! Dyphestive!" He fell out of his wagon when he stood. "You're back!"

Everyone with two legs rushed over to Grey Cloak. They all shared big hugs and many cheek kisses.

Zanna was the last to hug her son. Her eyes watered.

"You escaped the Nether Realm? Or is this you from another time?" Grey Cloak asked.

"I escaped. Gossamer and I had a plan."

"Thanks for telling me. I was ready to come for you."

"I know, but I thought I would give you some rest."

"It's time to celebrate!" Razor shouted. "Break out the best of Littleton! It's not great. It's not even good. But it'll do!"

Grey Cloak was about to share the details of their journey to Nalzambor when a roar like rolling thunder carried across the sky and shook all of them in their boots. The birds nesting in the nearby bush scattered into the field and the sky.

"Roooaaar!"

2

"THUNDERBOLTS! WHAT WAS THAT?" Razor asked as he cleaned out one of his ears with a finger.

The ghostly form of the wizard Dalsay appeared in their midst and answered, "That was Black Frost."

Everyone scoured the skies.

"He's not close," Dalsay continued. "His dragon call came from his temple in Dark Mountain."

"He sounds angry," Grey Cloak said.

"Or hungry," Dyphestive added.

"We suspect he knows," Dalsay replied. "We picked up on Black Frost's bellow at the northern tower, which sent a signal here."

Zanna came forward and asked, "You said he knows? Black Frost knows what?"

Dalsay looked at the blood brothers.

"So much for a welcome-back celebration," Grey Cloak said with a sheepish smile. "I haven't even had a moment to explain what happened on our journey. We retrieved all five of the Thunderstones, but we ran into a situation."

"What situation?" Zanna asked.

A lone figure with locks of long, wavy blond hair exited the tower.

Zanna drew a blade.

Gossamer jumped to his feet. His eyes flashed with energy. "What is she doing here?"

Grey Cloak stepped in front of them and said, "That's the situation I need to explain. Please, give me a moment."

Zora stood nearby with her arms crossed. "This will prove interesting."

Magnolia strolled up to the group with a confident, friendly look on her beautiful face. "Hello, everybody."

Several members of Talon exchanged confused looks.

Gossamer's jaw muscles clenched. "She is evil."

"She's an ally now. You have to believe me," Grey Cloak said as he nodded at Magnolia. "She helped save us from an attack by her brother, Dirklen."

"He's not in the tower, is he?" Zanna said.

"No. When we recovered the Thunderstones, Dirklen had the Stone of Transport. He used it to save himself, return to Black Frost, and warn him of our plans."

"That's the theory anyway," Dyphestive added.

Crane approached Magnolia and eyeballed her from head to toe. "Are you married?" he asked.

"No," she answered with a charming smile then leaned down and pinched his chubby cheeks. "Are you?"

"Our plans?" Zanna asked loudly, furrowing her brow. "What does he know about our plans?"

"Dirklen knows about the Apparatus of Ruune," Grey Cloak said. "No doubt Black Frost will try to stop us from building it." He approached his mother. "And as I saw when we returned, we have the Helm of the Dragons as well, thanks to you. It gives us an edge. Black Frost won't know about that."

Zanna shook her head. "I wouldn't be so sure. It's best we assume he does. After all, Utlas the Speaker is a worm. I have no doubt he'd roll over."

Grey Cloak took a breath. "Zooks. You're right. But two great weapons are better than one, assuming we can protect them."

Dalsay floated a foot higher and said, "I bear more ill news."

"It gets worse?" Razor asked.

"Black Frost's forces are laying siege to the Wizard Watch tower in Ugrad. They aim to destroy it. And they're marching into any territory that has not been taken. The Day of Doom is upon us, and a fleet of Riskers is flying south, our way."

"So this is it. The final battle begins." Razor patted the steel handles on his hips. "I'm ready."

"What are we going to do?" Zora asked, worried. "Can we even build the Apparatus of Ruune without a fifth stone? Is the Helm of the Dragon able to control Black Frost?"

"That's what we're about to find out." Grey Cloak spun on his heel. "I'm going back into the tower to consult with Tatiana and get a closer look at the matter. Anyone who cares to join me, feel welcome."

"I'll stay here," Anya said. "I need to catch up with Cinder. We'll patrol the skies from here. You can have your towers."

Grey Cloak moved toward the tower with Zanna and Zora. He shouted behind him, "We'll be back!"

Dyphestive waved an arm and said, "Don't get any inspirations and go anywhere without me."

"Or me," Streak said. He had joined with some of his brothers and sisters, bumping noses and horns with them. "Come on, siblings. Let me tell you about the dragons in Nalzambor. They're beautiful."

Inside the Time Mural chamber, Tatiana the sorceress sat on a pewter throne beside Nath. He held the instructions to build the Apparatus of Ruune, which Brenwar Boulderguild had given them. His brow furrowed.

"What's wrong?" Grey Cloak asked.

Tatiana turned their way and said, "We can't build it."

"Pardon? What do you mean, 'we can't build it'? Is it because we don't have the Stone of Transport?"

"No," Nath said as he scratched his head, "that isn't the problem. It takes at least three stones to power it, but in this situation, five would be more ideal." He pointed a scaly finger at the lettering on the plans. "I've built swords but not anything this, er, technical."

"What is he saying?" Zanna asked.

Tatiana answered, "He's saying the instructions are too advanced for him. They are too advanced for me. And Dalsay has looked at it as well."

"Black Frost and his forces are on his way. How are we supposed to build it?" Grey Cloak asked.

Nath fingered the etchings on the instructions. "This is dwarven craft. Only dwarves can build it."

"I know a dwarf who might do."

"That's assuming dwarves in this world can interpret the work of dwarves in another." Nath rolled up the parchment and handed it to Grey Cloak. "What do you have in mind?"

"Dwarf Skull, here we come."

3

Dalsay returned and joined Tatiana on the Pedestal of Power. As her fingers massaged the air above the gemstones in the pedestal, a new image started to form in the Time Mural's archway.

The myriad of gems embedded in the arch's stones began to brighten, and the wall behind it twisted and swirled.

Tatiana said, "From here, we can spy on the activities outside all the other towers. This is the view from the Ugrad tower, south of Dark Mountain. The one Gossamer and Zanna used on their return. The Black Guard is staging a siege."

Grey Cloak moved away from the thrones and joined the others before the archway. The view swept over the bleak land of Ugrad, which was leagues of steppes like grassy wheat, jagged hills, and stone. He tilted his head. "Is that a catapult?"

"Catapults." Zanna pointed at the thousands of marching soldiers circling the tower. From a distance of no more than fifty yards, they'd built their siege camp. Behind them, on the rocky roads that twisted over hills, catapults rolled along, pulled by stout soldiers. "I count a score of them."

Zora brushed her fingers over the strap of her satchel. "What are they trying to do? Knock the tower down? What good will that do if they think we're in there, but we're in here?"

Dalsay moved between them and said, "It will do little good at first. We're far from harm, but the towers are connected. Black Frost will try to destroy them all, one by one. As one falls, the others will weaken."

"And that will destroy the Time Mural," Grey Cloak said.

"Yes." Dalsay nodded. "But do we still need the Time Mural? It has proved fatal. Now that all have returned, perhaps it is best that it's destroyed."

Grey Cloak rubbed his chin. "We might need it."

"Portals like this give Black Frost his power," Tatiana said as she passed her fingers over the glowing stones. "It can only leave our world and others in danger. And it is not your choice. It is the decision of the Wizard Watch, of which only a few are left."

"Who? You, Dalsay, and Gossamer?" Grey Cloak asked. "I think others should have a say in it."

"We won't make a hasty decision," Tatiana assured him. "For now, we need the Time Mural to monitor Black Frost's actions. But time is pressing. He's coming."

Dragons whizzed across the mural with Riskers riding on their backs. They were a thunder of middlings led by a grand.

From the corner of his eye, Grey Cloak caught the twinkle of the Helm of the Dragons. It sat on a small pedestal between the mural and where Dalsay hovered. He walked through Dalsay and picked up the helm. The dragon charms that decorated the helm were as smooth as polished glass. Each one winked with light when his fingers brushed over it, and his blood warmed. "We need to strike first."

Tatiana gave him a curious look. "What do you mean?"

"It's time to send Black Frost a message. Give him something to think about and buy more time." He turned to Zora. "Do you think she can control those dragons from here?"

"Here is the same as being there. I don't see why not," Tatiana said. "But the helm is designed to be wielded by naturals, not ordinary people." She looked at Zora. "No offense, sister."

"I'm not offended." Zora grimaced at the helm. "I felt my mind rip apart that last time I used it, and it hurts to think about it. Besides, shouldn't Sky Riders control dragons?" She shoved Zanna. "Perhaps you can be further useful. After all, you stole it."

Zanna grinned. "I did, didn't I?"

"Well, we don't want to tip our hand too much," Grey Cloak said. "Do all the towers have a defense system like the one in the Wilds of Arrowwood?"

Tatiana nodded. "They do, thanks to the underlings, but it will drain our energy. Energy we might need later."

"We don't need to use much. We only need to send them a warning. Put them on their heels."

"The foundation of the Wizard Watch is deep. They are nearly impossible to take down," Dalsay said as he floated toward the thrones and sat. "The stones are mystically fused together. But the defense systems can be operated from these chairs."

Nath raised an eyebrow as he looked down at the mystical etchings and small illuminated gems in the arm of his chair. "Fascinating. I wondered what these strange buttons were for."

Grey Cloak handed the helm to his mother. "Let's see if we can spook them. Aim for those catapults."

She nodded. "I'd love to."

Gossamer rushed into the chamber, panting. "Come quickly! We have a visitor!"

"Who?" Grey Cloak asked.

"Dirklen."

Silence fell over the chamber.

Then Grey Cloak said, "Once we're outside, close down everything. Whatever you do, don't let him in."

4

Outside the tower, Dirklen stood surrounded by Talon as well as the dragons. His wavy locks of blond hair had been slicked back and hung down to his broad shoulders. The sleeves of his black dragon armor were gone, but the metal gauntlets remained. He had Crane in a headlock, and the old man's face was beet red as he struggled.

"Where did he come from?" Grey Cloak asked Gossamer as they approached.

"He appeared out of thin air," the elven sorcerer replied.

"Dirklen, stop this now!" Magnolia pleaded. The creases in her face were deep with worry. Tears shone in her eyes. "What's happened to you?"

"Me? What's wrong with you, sister? You betrayed me! You broke the oath between brother and sister." Dirklen sneered. He whisked a dagger out of his scabbard and spun it in the air. "All of you are dead, though you don't know it. But I think I'll start with the old one."

"That wouldn't surprise me one bit," Grey Cloak said. "You never did like a fair fight."

Dirklen shuffled around. His eyes burned with green fire, and the emerald Stone of Transport was embedded in the chest of his armor. "Ah, there's the one I'm looking for. I'm going to enjoy killing all of your friends while you watch and suffer." He pointed his dagger at all of them. "Then I'll kill you, one piece at a time."

The Cloak of Legends pulsed a warning, and Grey Cloak stopped. This wasn't the Dirklen he knew. The man before him was inches taller and more muscular. Traces of green energy crawled across his body, like spiders speeding across a web.

"Is that what you really want, Dirklen? Death? Revenge?" Grey Cloak asked.

"No, I want victory. Domination. And the likes of you weaklings stand in the way of that!"

Streak joined Grey Cloak. "What are we waiting for? Let's waste this guy. He's an idiot."

Dirklen tightened his grip on Crane. The pudgy old man gasped and kicked.

Magnolia rushed forward with her arms out. "No, brother! This isn't you." She clasped her hands and dropped to her knees. "Please don't do this. If you want to hurt anyone, hurt me. I was the one who betrayed you."

Dirklen softened his hold on Crane, and the old man sputtered and spat. Pointing his dagger at all of them, Dirklen said, "If any of you take one more step toward me, I will snap his neck. As for you, sister, do you really think I would kill my own flesh and blood?" He shrugged. "What sort of brother would that make me?"

The air prickled, and the hairs on Grey Cloak's neck rose.

Dirklen's bright eyes turned hot.

"Magnolia, move!" Grey Cloak warned her as he sprang forward.

Fire shot out of Dirklen's eyes, streaked toward Magnolia, and smashed into her chest, sending her skidding across the grass.

Grey Cloak groaned as bolts struck his cloak and knocked him to the ground. "Augh!" The folds of the Cloak of Legends swaddled him as Dirklen brought down more heat.

"What are you doing, fool? Trying to die on account of my sister? As I said, I'm saving you for last—*urk!*"

Dyphestive had bull-rushed Dirklen and knocked him down.

The fire in Dirklen's eyes dimmed. Gorva ripped Crane free of his grip, and he hurried away.

"Stay still," Dyphestive warned Dirklen as he locked his

fingers behind his neck in a full headlock and held him on the ground.

Razor snaked in and put the tip of his sword to Dirklen's throat. "You can breathe, but I wouldn't do anything else."

Dirklen scowled and asked, "You think you can stop me?" He scanned the group. "You have no idea what you're in for. Go ahead. Cut me and see if I die."

With a shrug, Razor replied, "If you insist."

"No," Dyphestive ordered. "We don't do that."

Dirklen gave a haughty chuckle. "And that's why you will lose." He started to force his head back.

Dyphestive's arms bulged, his face flushed, and his jaw muscles clenched as he shoved Dirklen's head downward. "Don't make me break your neck."

"Oaf! Your strength is that of a gnat compared to mine." Dirklen snapped his head back, hitting Dyphestive's chin. He broke free, and in one smooth motion, he smacked Razor's blade aside, jumped to his feet, drew his own sword, and pointed it at Razor's chest.

Wide-eyed, Razor said with his arms up, "That was fast."

"This is faster." Dirklen stabbed Razor in the chest.

"Urk!" Razor fell to his knees, clutching his chest.

Many gasped.

Gorva screamed. "No!" She rushed to Razor's side and cradled him in her arms.

With eyes as big as saucers and his skin turning pale, Razor said, "I didn't see that coming, my love."

"You're a monster!" Zora shouted at Dirklen. She hurried to Gorva's side.

Grey Cloak returned to his feet with the Rod of Weapons charging in his hands. He, Dyphestive, Anya, Shannon, and Tinison circled the villain with weapons drawn. Behind them were the dragons: Cinder, Streak, Feather, Slicer, and Slick.

Streak said, "It's time to end this jerk!"

Dirklen put his hands on his hips, tossed his head back, and laughed. Then he put his sword away and said, "Come, ugly dragon. I want to see you try."

Streak advanced.

Grey Cloak stepped in front of him. "Don't take the bait."

Razor gasped for breath, with the light in his eyes fading. The blade master was dying. More would die if they attacked. Grey Cloak could see it in Dirklen's eyes.

He doused the Rod of Weapons and set it down. "Dirklen, we surrender."

5

DIRKLEN BLINKED, and the triumphant scowl on his face vanished. "What do you mean, you 'surrender'?"

With his hands up, Grey Cloak backed away from his weapon. "I don't want any more bloodshed. We give up. Tell us what you want. You want something, don't you?"

"Grey Cloak, are you mad?" Anya asked.

Everyone appeared shocked, disappointed, and confused.

I have to defuse the situation. Dirklen wants a fight. A reason to kill. And my gut tells me he's only toying with us. I need to buy more time and find a weakness.

"Are you playing games with me again, Grey Cloak? Is that what this is about? You hope to catch me off guard and attack," Dirklen said. "Well, you fooled me once and sent me to that dung hole called Bish. You won't fool me again."

"He saved you from hanging from a noose, brother!" Magnolia said as she climbed back to her feet. Her breastplate armor was scorched black. "You were remorseful then. You should be thankful now that you're alive."

"Then, I didn't wield the power I do now." Dirklen clenched his metal-coated fist, and it burned like green flames. "I am invincible, filled with only a taste of Black Frost's power! I can do whatever I wish." He pointed his fist at Cinder, and a blast of mystic energy shot out.

The fiery ball smote Cinder in the chest, knocking him backward, and the grand dragon fell on his wings.

"Cinder!" Anya shrieked.

"Father!" Fenora the grand and Feather the middling said as they rushed to their father's side.

"Dirklen, stop this!" Grey Cloak pleaded. "Please!"

I've learned one thing. Power provided by Black Frost. Check.

"Oh, quit whining, Grey Cloak. I prefer your snarky side better." Dirklen's eyes flashed. "It makes me angry, and when I feel angry, I feel strong."

Keep him talking. Let Zora work on Razor before he dies.

Grey Cloak moved away from Razor and asked, "What do you want? Perhaps we can make a deal." *Appeal to his enormous ego.* "Let us live, and I'll give you what you came for."

"What makes you think I came for anything? My orders are simple. Seek and destroy you."

"Certainly you want the weapons that can destroy Black Frost," Grey Cloak replied.

"Grey, what are you doing?" Dyphestive asked.

"Oh-ho, so you want to make an exchange? Now why would you do that?" Dirklen rubbed the whiskers on his chin. "Do you hope to catch me off guard? Perhaps you plan to move back in time and undo what you've done." His gaze flicked toward the Wizard Watch. "I know they're watching me. Waiting to make a move. I won't be fooled so easily." The corners of his mouth turned up in a wry smile. "Perhaps they need something to think about." He winked at Grey Cloak.

Dirklen vanished then reappeared beside his sister and grabbed her, and they both disappeared.

"Whoa!" Streak said with his yellow eyes searching. "That was slick!"

"No, I'm Slick," Slick said.

"Zora, how's Razor?" Grey Cloak asked.

"I fed him a vial, but it might be too late."

A woman screamed high in the sky.

Dirklen hovered in the air at the top of the tower. His sister was wrapped up in his arms—until he dropped her.

Magnolia clawed at the air and screamed.

Streak launched himself into the air, saying, "I've got this!" He swooped under Magnolia when she was halfway to the ground, and she clung to him.

Dirklen reappeared in their midst and laughed. He tapped the Thunderstone on his chest and said, "I can do this at will." He drew his dagger. "I wonder who I'll torment next."

Sword in hand, a red-hot Anya said, "Torment me, fool!"

"Why not?" Dirklen shrugged and vanished.

Anya spun around.

Everyone searched the land and sky.

"Stay close. Form a battle ring," Dyphestive ordered.

They marched back-to-back, forming a close circle, and the dragons formed a ring around them, but Dirklen popped up behind Fenora, a sassy grand dragon with jade-colored scales, and stabbed her in the haunch.

Fenora belted out a roar, and fire shot from her mouth. She spun around, swinging her tail, but Dirklen was gone.

"Duck!" Grey Cloak said as Fenora's tail passed over his head. He was quick, but Shannon and Tinison weren't quick enough, and they went flying into the high grasses.

"Ahahaha!" the power-mad Dirklen laughed. He stood thirty yards away, rubbing his hands together. "This is going to be a delight. And I love your ring of honor. Though I fear its simplicity." Bolts shot out of his eyes and bore down on them.

They scattered.

Grey Cloak poked his head up. Dirklen was gone again.

"Where is he?" Streak asked. "I don't see him. I swear I'm going to snack on that human!"

Dyphestive's expression made him look as lost as Grey Cloak.

The moment Dyphestive shrugged, Dirklen popped up behind him and rammed a sword straight into his back.

Dyphestive fell over like a tree and had a glassy stare in his eyes.

"Oh, it looks like I got the donkey skull right in the heart," Dirklen mocked. He tilted his head to one side. "I think he's dead."

Grey Cloak's heart skipped. He'd lost sight of his brother's body in the tall grasses. All he could see was Dirklen's gloating face as his flaming eyes ignited for another attack.

"Who shall be next?" Dirklen pulled his sword free. "A dragon, perhaps?" He swung his gaze toward Feather. "How about the pinkish one?"

A bolt of lightning streaked down from the sky, followed by a clap of thunder. The bolt blasted into Dirklen and crushed him into the ground.

Anya stood in the field with her sword pointed at the

sky and her eyes flickering like campfires. She wore an angry scowl.

Grey Cloak started toward his brother, but Dalsay appeared before him. "No, don't."

"I have to help Dyphestive," Grey Cloak replied, anguished.

"No, you have to help the rest before he destroys them all," Dalsay warned him. "You must distract Dirklen and get the others into the safety of the tower. There, he cannot enter." He glanced over his shoulder. Dirklen had started to rise. "The Wizard Watch is the only choice. We will do what we can to bring others in. Tatiana is working on it, but it won't be easy. No matter what, we cannot let him inside." He eyed the tower's entrance, which was closed. "Watch for an opening." Dalsay vanished.

"Streak, did you hear that?" Grey Cloak asked.

Magnolia climbed off Streak's back. "I'll keep trying to reason with Dirklen. I know him. He's listening but being stubborn."

"Stubborn or not, we can't take any more chances. He's already tried to kill you twice." He kicked the Rod of Weapons into his hands. "It's time to give him the fight he's been looking for." He twirled it around with a flip of his wrist and aimed at Dirklen. "Goy! Dirklen. I have something for you!" He shot balls of energy that zipped across the prairie and struck Dirklen in the chest. "How's that taste?"

Dirklen stood his ground, put a fist on his hip, and brushed his chest with his other hand. "Like victory to me, worm. Taste this!" He shot energy from his eyes.

Grey Cloak ducked.

Magnolia dived too. She continued to plead with her brother. "Stop this madness, you spoiled child!" She rushed toward him with her sword drawn.

"Your voice makes my ears tire. Enough of this."

Slick and Slicer dropped from the sky, swooping in from opposite directions.

Dirklen turned at the last moment toward Slicer. The Stone of Transport's inner light flickered, and he disappeared.

Slick and Slicer roared, and they crashed head-on. Both lay still in a heap of scales.

Gossamer was tending to Crane near the wagon. Both of them vanished.

"Dragons, take to the sky. It will be harder for him to attack you there."

"You heard him!" Fenora said. "To the winds!"

Every able dragon took flight, but Cinder, Slick, and Slicer stayed on the ground.

Grey Cloak eyed Gorva, Zora, and Razor. "When the tower door opens, get Razor inside, but not before Dirklen reappears and we engage him. The same for Shannon and Tinison. I don't know how many others Tatiana can teleport in."

Grey Cloak turned in a slow circle as he made his way toward his brother. "Where are you, Dirklen?" He slipped off his boots. "What trick do you want to play this time?" He noticed Zanna crouched by the wagon with one of her swords drawn. "Any ideas?"

"No, I was hoping you'd think of something," she said as her gaze slid over the landscape. "A shame you left the Thunderstones inside. I have a feeling we could have used them."

"I did notice one detail. The Thunderstone winks before he moves," Grey Cloak offered. "We need to get close enough to remove it from him."

"Easier said than done," Magnolia interjected. She shook her sword and raised her voice. "Where are you, brother? Don't be a coward! Come out!"

"There he is!" Zanna pointed at the tower's rooftop.

Dirklen sat with his legs dangling over the ledge. He waved.

"He really is toying with us," Grey Cloak said. He waved his enemy down. With a heavy heart, he backed toward Dyphestive. "Cover me."

"I'll try," Magnolia said.

He hadn't made it halfway to Dyphestive before Dirklen blinked out of sight. He reappeared in the wagon and kicked Zanna in the back of the head.

Zanna lost her sword and fell face-first to the ground.

"Oof! I bet that hurt. I think I heard her skull crack,"

Dirklen said. He hopped out of the wagon, sword in hand, and cut across the grass from side to side. He set his gaze on Anya. "You're fair with a sword, aren't you? How about a duel? Me versus you? I promise I won't kill you too quickly."

Anya stormed forward. "I'd be happy to feed you my sword."

"No, Anya," Grey Cloak said. "He's only baiting you."

"I don't care!"

Dirklen pointed his blade at Grey Cloak and the others and said, "No interference. This is a fair challenge, dragon rider against dragon rider. To the death." He turned back to Anya. "Do you accept?"

Anya buckled on her helmet and spoke through her teeth. "With glee."

"Tut-tut," Dirklen said as he waved his sword at Grey Cloak. "Your brother's dead. Now, give us some space, and when it's over, if you're lucky, I might let you dig all their graves." He cast a glance at the spot where Gossamer and Crane had been. "Where did they go?"

Grey Cloak answered, "As far away from you as possible?"

Dirklen eyed the dragons circling in the skies. "Smart move." He turned his attention to Anya and nodded.

She attacked.

7

___

ANYA AND DIRKLEN'S blades collided in a fierce dance of flashing steel. Against his enhanced abilities, she held her own, staying in front of him and keeping his back to the tower.

Out of the corner of his eye, Grey Cloak watched the tower's slab door crack open.

Gorva and Zora hooked Razor by the arms, stayed low, and dragged the dying man toward the gap.

Grey Cloak stayed within Dirklen's line of vision, not wanting his head to turn. *Keep his focus on us.*

He caught Shannon and Tinison limping as quickly as they could toward the opening.

In a matter of minutes, Dirklen had taken down Cinder, Slick, and Slicer. He'd forced Fenora, Feather, and Streak into the skies. Dyphestive was possibly dead, and Zanna was knocked out cold. Only Grey Cloak, Magnolia, and Anya were on their feet, with Anya battling for her life.

I have to help her somehow.

Grey Cloak moved toward the battle.

"Stay in your place! This is a matter of honor!" Anya said as she blocked one sword stroke and ducked under another. "I will win this!"

"No, you won't!" Dirklen's sword weaved through the air like a striking cobra. "I'm stronger!"

Their weapons clashed. *Bang!*

"Faster!"

Clang!

Dirklen's voice grew deeper and more resonant. "The finest swordsman! The greatest dragon rider of all!" He unleashed a flurry of thrusts and chops, hacking at her with vigor. *Crash! Bang! Clang!*

Anya parried with both hands on her sword grip. Dirklen batted her sword aside, only for her to spring back and block again. She gave ground, shuffling backward with her brow furrowed.

Shannon and Tinison dived through the gap in the door as it started to close, finally sealing them inside.

But Grey Cloak still couldn't breathe easily.

Anya was outmatched and would only last as long as Dirklen would let her.

"I've heard so many tales about the great Anya!" Dirklen mocked. "Once again, I can't help but feel unimpressed." He withdrew his attack and lowered his guard. "Take a moment. Catch your breath." He started to turn toward the tower.

Anya charged with her sword cocked over her shoulder and brought it down hard.

Dirklen blocked, and droplets of energy flew off their swords. They came nose to nose, and he stole a quick kiss.

She jumped back and spat. "You disgust me!"

"Don't fret, darling. You'll be kissing worms soon enough."

Anya wiped her mouth on her metal sleeve. "I'd rather kiss them than a dirty dog like you."

"All to be arranged soon enough." He waved his sword at her. "Come on, Anya the legend. Let's finish this dance. It begins to bore me."

"Uuugh!" She charged.

Dirklen lashed out, and Anya ducked. The blade of his sword knocked her helmet off. She stumbled to the ground and landed on her knees, gasping.

Grey Cloak had never seen Anya so winded. He watched in horror as Dirklen advanced. "Get up, Anya!"

Dirklen grinned. "Get up. Stay down. It makes no difference. You're dead already."

Anya fought her way back to her feet. Her head was bleeding. She blinked hard, faced Dirklen, and kissed her blade. "If this is it, this is it. But you'll never win."

"I beg to disagree."

Magnolia cried, "Enough of this madness, brother! We've offered you everything. Let us live!"

Keeping his back to his sister, he said, "It's too late. Unlike you, there was never any good in me." He sped toward Anya as swiftly as the wind and knocked her sword from her fingers then spun around in a full circle. The bright steel of his sword flashed like a sickle and tore clear through Anya's body.

Grey Cloak's stomach sank into his toes.

Dirklen's momentum twisted him halfway around. His head snapped back toward Anya. She was gone.

"What trickery is this?" He glared at Grey Cloak and Magnolia, his nostrils flaring. "Where did she go? The tower?"

Grey Cloak smirked. "No victory for you, but I'll be happy to dance with you."

"Ah, is that your game? Hide in the tower? There is nowhere you can run. Nowhere you can hide, weaklings!" He pounded his chest. "I will tear open those doors and bring your entire world down." He almost stumbled on Dyphestive's big body. "Just like his!"

Dyphestive's ham-sized fist shot up, and he hammered Dirklen right in the beans.

With widening eyes, Dirklen groaned. "Oof!" His sword fell from his fingers.

"Yes!" Grey Cloak pounced.

Before he could get to him, Dyphestive swallowed

Dirklen in his mighty arms and crushed him in a bear hug.

"Get the stone!" Grey Cloak said.

There was no mistaking the painful, stunned look on Dirklen's face. He looked like he'd swallowed an anvil.

"Dyphestive, move your meaty arms! I can't get to the Thunderstone," Grey Cloak pleaded.

"Understood." Dyphestive shifted his arms, exposing the stone.

Grey Cloak fastened his fingers on the jewellike rock. "Dirty acorns, it's anchored in there tight."

"Let me try." Dyphestive fumbled over the spot, digging and prying at the rock. "I think I can get it."

"What are you doing?" Dirklen managed to say.

Magnolia took his face in her palms and drew his gaze to hers. "Be calm, brother. We're trying to aid you."

"I'm burning from the waist down. What happened?" Dirklen's lips tightened. "No. I know what happened. That oaf socked me in the nanoos!"

Grey Cloak used a small dagger to try to dig the stone out. "Brother, we're running out of time," he warned him under his breath.

Dirklen screamed. At the same time, he and Dyphestive both disappeared.

"Oh no," Grey Cloak said as a shadow moved over him.

He and Magnolia looked up to see Dyphestive plummeting down.

"Jump!"

8

Like an anvil, Dyphestive hit the ground face-first with a thud. His body made an inches-deep impression in the dirt. "Auugh."

Grey Cloak and Magnolia hurried to his side.

"Grab an arm," Grey Cloak said to her. "Nice landing, brother."

Dyphestive spat flower petals out of his mouth and looked up. "Did you see where he dropped me from?" They looked up. "I was kissing the clouds and trying to squeeze the blood out of him, and *poof*, he was gone again. Lucky this ground broke my fall."

As Grey Cloak helped his brother to his feet, he said, "Next time, shout a warning. You almost landed on me."

"Yes, well, I can't think of everything. After all, only moments ago, he ran his sword through me."

Dirklen reappeared between them and Crane's wagon, irritation showing on his face. "Why won't you die? Are you too stupid to die?"

"I'm not stupid," Dyphestive said as he brushed the grass from his shoulders. "Maybe you're too ignorant to kill me."

Solid beams of emerald light shot out of Dirklen's eyes and hit Dyphestive full force.

He was knocked off his feet and skipped across the grass.

Magnolia pleaded, "Why don't you take what these people have offered? Take it to Black Frost and be gone."

Let them squabble, Grey Cloak thought. *That gives me time to think up a most excellent plan. I can predict when he might transport, but I can't predict where he will go. Perhaps I can set up some bait.*

Zanna pushed herself up slowly, and he caught her eye.

He mouthed, "Be ready."

She nodded.

"You disgust me, Dirklen!" Magnolia yelled. She shook her fist at him. "I hope you die!"

"I won't die! But you will!" he screamed back.

"Mother, stay down!" Grey Cloak called.

Dirklen's gaze shifted to her. "Time to finish this!" He disappeared in the wink of an eyelash and reappeared by Zanna.

Her eyes narrowed, and she punched him in the

stomach with a dagger charged with wizard fire, pushing deep.

"Hurk!" Dirklen gasped loudly. His face paled, and his legs wobbled.

Grey Cloak and Magnolia charged.

Gasping for breath, Dirklen vanished a split second before they arrived.

Zanna still had her dagger. His blood sizzled on the blade. "I hit him good, but I don't think it was enough."

"No, but it was enough to scare him." He spotted Dyphestive rising from the ground. "Come on! We need to get inside before he comes back!"

A huff of hot air stirred their hair and clothing. Cinder rose and shook his head.

"Are you well?" Grey Cloak asked.

"Well enough. It felt like a storm giant had struck me." He nudged Slick and Slicer. "Get up, you two lazy hounds."

They stirred.

Streak landed close to Grey Cloak. "What now, boss?"

"Everyone, get inside. The time to hide has come. Call your brothers and sisters. We need to enter the Wizard Watch now. Dirklen's too dangerous for any of us to stay out here."

Grey Cloak grabbed the nightmare horse Charro by the reins. She snorted and clawed at the dirt.

"Come on, girl. I wouldn't forget about you. Crane would never forgive me."

Making haste, the entire group of men, women, and dragons entered the tower.

Grey Cloak waved them inside. "Hurry!"

The slab door descended just as Dirklen appeared outside. He locked eyes with Grey Cloak long enough to see him smirk and wave goodbye.

The door sealed, and something hit it. *Boom! Boom! Boom!*

"Lords of the Air, what is he doing out there?" Zanna asked.

Dalsay appeared. "You can get a better view from upstairs. Come."

Everyone gathered in the Time Mural chamber, where Razor was bandaged up and quite alive.

"I've been stabbed so many times that I can no longer count it on my fingers." He took a swig from a long black bottle of port. "Maybe I'm immortal."

"Your fortune is uncanny," Gorva said. She stood by his side, watching the image in the mural.

"And so is yours." Razor tried to kiss her, but she moved away. He made smooching sounds. "Don't worry, love. I fully respect your unwillingness to display public affection."

Gorva rolled her eyes.

Through a window, the rest of the company watched Dirklen try to destroy the tower using his fists and fire from his eyeballs. The floor trembled from the impact.

"How can he have such power?" Gossamer asked. "It's that of a titan."

"He's imbued with the same energy Black Frost has stolen from my home," Nath said from the throne on the right in a scratchy voice. "I can only imagine that Black Frost's strength is one hundred times that. I guess we have a much better perspective of what we're dealing with."

"Tatiana, are you certain this tower can hold against him?" Zora asked. "I see chips of stone flying."

"It will hold against the likes of him so long as the other towers stand. This stronghold is much more than rock and stone." Tatiana turned her lovely eyes on Grey Cloak. "What is our next course of action, fearless leader?"

"Give me a moment..."

Everyone sighed, got comfortable, and said, "He'll think of something."

9

———

OUTSIDE THE TOWER, Dirklen's rage had cooled. He stood in the campground, talking to himself and waiting, vanishing for several moments before coming back again.

"He must be informing Black Frost," Zanna said. She rubbed the knot on the back of her head. "He's planning something."

"Well, so are we." Grey Cloak fluffed his cloak and said, "Tatiana, we can exit this tower into any other location, can't we?"

"Of course. That's the design. Wizards were never very big on traveling. There is one in Crow Valley, near Dwarf Skull, if that's what you were thinking."

He nodded. "We need to take the apparatus's plans to Dwarf Skull. Hopefully, there Rhonna can help us. At the same time, I think it would be best for the dragons to return to Safe Haven. The time has come to armor them for the final fight. And we can use the Eye of the Sky Rider to get a better view of Black Frost's activities. "

Dyphestive punched his fists together. "I'm all for that."

"Regardless of the tower's location," Tatiana warned him, "Black Frost will certainly have eyes on it." Her hands gyrated over the pedestal of stones, and the image in the archway began to shift. "Let's have a look."

The landscape changed from the sprawling prairies to hard-packed clay and rocks with sparse vegetation. The winds swept the dust across the landscape, and tall cacti with needles longer than men's fingers bent. Slowly, the image moved around the perimeter of the southern tower.

"Looks safe to me," Razor remarked. "Whoever goes had better take a lot of water, but I volunteer to stay here and secure the wine."

"What do you think, Dyphestive?" Grey Cloak asked.

His brother rubbed his jaw, raised an eyebrow, and said, "I wouldn't mind paying Rhonna a visit. I'll take the plans and go."

"Here's what I'm thinking," Grey Cloak said. "We need to keep Dirklen convinced that we're operating out of this tower. Keep his attention. We might even have to make an appearance on the outside to give him something to think about. Launch an attack."

"Perhaps capture him," Anya suggested. "Though I'd rather he'd be dead. I want to fight him on equal terms."

The Thunderstones, sitting by the foot of the empty throne, caught Grey Cloak's eye. He snapped his fingers. "Nath, can we use these stones in the same manner Dirklen has?"

Nath smiled. "I like the way you think. But it's dangerous. Dirklen's abilities are boosted by Black Frost. His body can handle it, but I cannot predict the outcome for anyone else. They aren't designed to be used by a single entity, though wizards have been the most successful in manipulating their qualities." He casually flipped his fingers upward, and all four Thunderstones rose into the air.

"Your charming friend throwing a tantrum outside wields the green Stone of Transport," Nath continued. Each marble-like stone shone as he spoke of it. "The yellow stone is power, pink gives the user the ability to command, much like your dragon charms, orange enhances sight in many ways, and blue offers elemental powers." The stones formed a ring. "Any three together can tear apart the foundations of a city. All five, well, who knows the sort of devastation they can bring. That's the purpose behind the Apparatus of Ruune. Its unique design can harness the awesome power of the Thunderstones. But if you use them individually, I warn you, tread lightly. Such power is dangerously addictive. You only need to look at Dirklen to see for yourself."

"You can say that again," a sad-faced Magnolia muttered. "Is there any hope for him?"

"There is always hope for anybody," Nath replied politely.

Boom!

The entire tower shook.

"Whoa!" Razor screamed.

"Zooks!" Grey Cloak exclaimed as the floor quaked beneath his bare feet. "Was that Dirklen?"

"I don't think so." Tatiana shifted the mural's image away from the wasteland of Crow Valley in Sulter Slay to the grasslands near the town of Littleton. Dirklen remained in the camp, pacing and muttering angrily.

The tower shook again.

Boom!

"The siege begins in Ugrad," Tatiana said.

The mural changed to the cold steppes in the north, where Black Frost's armies had gathered. The catapults had been pulled into the tower's perimeter. Globe-like rocks bigger than large pumpkins were loaded into the catapults' slings. Men in robes set fire to them using their hands, and the strange rocks burned bright red.

"What are those globes?" Grey Cloak asked.

"They're mortars filled with black dust," Magnolia answered. "They are designed to destroy rocks as well as magic."

"Does it work?" he asked Tatiana.

A catapult launched, and a great ball of red fire whizzed through the sky then struck the tower. *Boom!*

"Apparently," Tatiana replied. "Or we wouldn't feel it. It's time to defend ourselves. It might take ten hits, or it might take one hundred, but we have no choice but to try to stop it."

More catapults were being pulled to the front lines and loaded. There were at least two dozen.

Grey Cloak jumped into one of the thrones and said, "Someone tell me how to work this thing." He studied the buttons on the armrests. "We need to stop this, and we need to stop it now."

Boom!

10

GOSSAMER MOVED to Grey Cloak's side and offered, "If you'd be so inclined, I would be happy to guide you through the controls, if not overtake them." He pushed a button, and a little stick popped up. "This aims the tower's weapon, and this button will activate it."

Grey Cloak pushed a gemstone button. "Impressive. How do I know what I'm aiming at?"

"Do you see the green circles with crosshairs?" Gossamer asked. "That's where the weapon is aimed to fire. When you're ready, press this button on the other arm."

A bolt of energy sizzled away from the image in the mural and blew a catapult to smithereens. Black Guards were flung into the air, and a gaping hole smoked in the landscape.

Nath laughed. "This is more like it, for an old warrior

like me." He moved the red circle of his sight and pushed the button. Another catapult exploded into little bits and pieces.

Every member of Talon cheered.

Nath let out his own quiet "Wahoo! This brings back memories."

Grey Cloak stiffened, took aim, and said, "Well, I'm not going to let you hog all the glory. Taste this, Black Guard!"

A succession of shots from the tower's cannons turned the catapults into hunks of burning wood.

"Thunderbolts! Let me try that!" Razor said. "It's not my style, but it looks like fun!"

Catapults exploded, and Black Guards scattered. They died in bits and pieces of metal and flesh.

"Ease off," Tatiana warned them. "The towers don't have limitless power. The more you use, the weaker the tower becomes. Pace yourself."

Grey Cloak lifted his finger from the trigger. "How long should we wait between shots?"

"I can't measure the drain. Perhaps we need less fire-power, and aim for the loads they put in the weapon." Tatiana worked behind the pedestal. "Give me some time."

"They're maneuvering," Dyphestive said. He pointed at the mural. "Look!"

Riskers led their dragons to the ground, where they were loaded with catapult globes and flew away.

"Where'd they go?" Zora asked.

Boom!

"That sounded like they hit the roof. They're trying to blow a hole through the top!" Dyphestive said.

"We can't let that happen," Grey Cloak replied. "Nath, work with me. We need to chase them down."

"The tower works like a turret. It will spin all the way around," Tatiana said. "One of you needs to guide it while the other aims the cannons."

"I'll drive. You fire!" Nath said.

The image moved faster, chasing the dragons.

Grey Cloak landed his pointer on a Risker. "Tatiana, can I shoot?"

"Take the shot!"

Crane's face was a mask of rage. He clenched his fist and said, "Fire!"

Grey Cloak chuckled as he hit the button and blew the dragon and his rider out of the sky. The creature exploded, and fiery masses of flesh and scales rained down.

Crane gave him a thumbs-up. "Do it again!" Like a snarling wolf, he said, "Fire!"

Two more Riskers were blasted out of the air. At the same time, more catapults were loaded and launched.

The walls shook. *Boom! Boom! Boom!*

"There're too many," Grey Cloak said as he fired another shot at one of the catapults. "We need more weapons."

"We don't have any more," Tatiana said, frowning. She

looked between the pedestal and the mural. "As I said, the more you fire, the weaker the tower becomes. We need another way to stop this."

Razor pulled his sword, and Gorva lifted her spear.

Dyphestive held up the Iron Sword. "How about a ground attack?"

"The three of you against an army? I don't think that's a good idea." Zanna picked up the Helm of the Dragons. "I have a better one. After all, this is the direction we were heading before." She eyed Zora. "Does anyone object?"

"It's all yours, as far as I'm concerned." Zora moved away. "I want no part of that."

Zanna turned to Grey Cloak. "Son?"

His eyes were focused on the mural. "I like the way you think. Do it."

"The moment of truth," Zanna uttered as she dropped the helm onto her head. She faced the mural. The light in the dragon charms embedded in the helmet started to build. Gasping, she flung her head back, and her limbs stiffened.

"Zanna, are you well?" Dyphestive asked.

"I'm fine. I need a moment. So many dragons. So many minds." Her gaze followed the flight of a dragon and its rider. She smiled. "Like clay in my fingers."

All of a sudden, one of the dragons dove toward the ground. Its rider fiercely pulled at the reins. At the last moment, the Risker jumped out of the saddle, and the middling dragon crashed into a catapult and exploded.

Two Riskers collided in midair. Dragons bucked their riders from their saddles and sent them plummeting toward the scrambling armies on the ground.

Other dragons rammed into the tower and skidded down. One by one, more dragons and catapults were wiped out.

"Watch this!" Zanna said with an undeniable thirst for power. She took control of a grand dragon. It skimmed the ground with flames spraying out of its mouth, turning catapults to ash and Black Guard soldiers into burning men running wild.

The battlefield burned. Black and white smoke covered the ground. Confused dragons wrestled against their riders and one another as if they'd gone mad.

Chaos reigned. Destruction was swift. The forces of Black Frost were thwarted.

The gem-studded helm burned like many candles on Zanna's head. She clenched her fists at her sides. "We are going to win this war! We will have victory! The Helm of the Dragons works!"

Grey Cloak caught Zora giving him a worried look. Goose bumps made the hairs on his arms rise.

The Helm of the Dragons grew brighter.

He moved off of the pedestal quickly and faced his mother. "Zanna, take it off."

She shook her head. Only the whites of her eyes showed. "He's coming!" she moaned.

"Who's coming?"

She pointed at the mural and in a hollow whisper said, "Black Frost!"

11

ZANNA RIPPED the Helm of the Dragons off her head. Her cheeks were rosy, and tiny droplets of sweat beaded on her face. "I felt him," she said as she gave Grey Cloak an awestruck look. "He's coming this way."

"Black Frost? Coming here?" Grey Cloak asked with a shake of his head. "That seems unlikely. Did you feel you could control him?"

"No. He was trying to control me. His mind is as immense as the rest of him. He spoke to me."

"What did he say?"

Zanna gulped. "He said, 'I know you. Succumb or die.'" She shivered. "I don't think we can stop him."

"Now isn't the time for doubt." Grey Cloak grabbed the helm and added, "This was created to stop him. If he's coming, now might be our only chance. Put it back on."

Her eyes grew wide. "What?"

"We'll need a distraction so that we can get an idea what we're up against. You can do it, Mother. There is no one better than you."

Zora tugged on his arm. "I don't think that's a good idea. The helm is strong. It eats at you. I can still hear dragons calling in my mind sometimes. The longer you bear it, the greater the burden."

"Then we will wait and see." Grey Cloak faced the mural. "After all, he cannot harm us so long as we remain in another tower. Correct, Tatiana?"

"We are safe only as long as we don't exit another tower. But if he's truly coming, it will be a bold thing to face him." Tatiana adjusted more stones. "He strikes quickly. I have no doubt in my mind he's coming to finish this."

Anya stepped closer. "I, for one, look forward to meeting the monster who destroyed my family face-to-face and feeding him my sword."

Far out on the horizon, where Dark Mountain loomed, great black wings appeared in the sky. It was a huge black dragon with blue eyes burning like cauldrons of fire. The shadow of his wings swallowed the hilltops.

"Monarchs of mercy." Crane moved beside Anya, put his arm around her waist, and said, "I think you're going to need a bigger sword."

"That can't be him. Nothing is so big," Razor said with

his head leaning to one side. "He looks bigger than a mountain."

"He *is* a mountain. Believe me. I've seen him for myself," Gossamer replied. "But I'd yet to see his wings fully spread out. He's even bigger than I imagined."

Black Frost was not alone. A host of dragons—little bigger than birds by comparison—flew alongside him. His body covered the ground in darkness. As he opened his mouth and roared, it felt like the entire world was shaking.

Tinison cowered behind one of the thrones and shouted, "It's over! No time to even dig a grave. We're finished."

Dyphestive joined Grey Cloak and said, "I never imagined he was so tremendous. We aren't even morsels to him."

Black Frost flew over the tower, and everyone got a full look at his face, which was broader than the tower itself. Great horns twisted behind his mammoth skull, which was covered in hard knots and spiny ridges. His belly scales were humongous plates like iron, and his tail was long enough to wrap around the tower like a snake.

He circled once and landed on the Black Guards who'd failed to escape his girth, crushing them. He sat on his haunches, folded his wings behind his back, and loomed over the tower.

The great dragon peered right at them. "I feel your eyes

on me. I can taste your fear. This is your last chance to surrender, weaklings."

Silence hung in the air for what seemed like an eternity. Like frightened rabbits, no one dared to move.

Even Grey Cloak felt the blood drain out of him as he finally stood face-to-face with the enemy he'd vowed to kill. The evil dragon took the strength right out of him. All of a sudden, his noble efforts seemed nothing but futile, and the inevitable conclusion became a dark blot in his mind.

Warmth passed through his fingertips, and he remembered he was still holding the Helm of the Dragons. Suddenly compelled, he put it on.

His mind expanded. The minds of the dragons were his. He called telepathically to the one he knew best, "Streak."

"Yes?" Streak answered. He was waiting on the main fountain level with his brothers and sisters.

"Be ready for anything. It's about to get ugly."

"Good. I'm all about some ugly."

Zora grabbed Grey Cloak's hands. "What are you trying to do?"

"I think it's time that Black Frost and I had a little talk, dragon to elf. He needs to know we mean business."

"Do you even know how to use the helm?"

"No, but I'll figure it out." Grey Cloak moved forward and used thoughts and words at the same time. "Hello,

Black Frost. I believe you've been looking for my brother and me. So glad you stopped by to chat. How can we help you?"

12

BLACK FROST SNORTED. "The little flea jests. How insolent." He glared right at them in the mural. "I offer you one last chance to serve. Only a fool would decline."

"Like all those fools you just landed on. I believe we'll pass. Perhaps it is you who should surrender," Grey Cloak suggested.

"I can feel you picking your way inside my head." Black Frost lifted a front claw and tapped his skull above an earhole. "Using the Helm of the Dragons to manipulate me. Perhaps, long ago, your toy would have worked, but I am far too strong to be controlled by your vessel now. Go ahead. Try to command anything of me. I invite you into my world."

Black Frost's mind might as well have been a hunk of steel. Grey Cloak forced his thoughts anyway.

You're feeling tired. Angry. Amused. Stomp your foot. Scratch your ear. Bark like a dog. Spread your wings.

Black Frost didn't bat an eyelash.

My, his mind is as hard as an anvil. A shame his cohorts aren't.

He commanded a grand dragon to fly into the side of Black Frost's head. The dragon hit Black Frost square in the jaw headfirst. Its neck broke, and it fell away as if it had hit stone.

"Your impudence is amusing, but I tire of your games, Grey Cloak!"

"Games? I love games. How about a hand of Birds?" He summoned several dragons and launched an attack on Black Frost.

Burn his eyes out!

Grand and middling dragons swarmed Black Frost like angry hornets. They spit dragon fire into his enormous eyes, crashed into them, and tried to claw them out.

Black Frost reared and gave a thunderous roar. He scraped the dragons away from his face as if they were rodents and crushed them with his claws. Man and dragon died. Others, he snatched from the air and swallowed whole. "Your stings are nothing to me! I cannot be harmed. Now, insects, feel my wrath!"

Black Frost opened his cavernous mouth filled with razor-sharp teeth. An eruption of blue-white flame came out and engulfed the image in the mural.

The air quickly turned hot.

"What's going on, Tatiana? Why can we feel the heat? We aren't even there," Zanna said.

"All the towers are connected. We stand in one as we stand in another." She combed her hair over her eyes. "This is not supposed to happen."

"The Pedestal of Power is overheating," Dalsay said. He pointed. "Look. Our powers are draining as we try to fend his attack off."

Gossamer joined them. "We need to cut away from Ugrad."

"You need to do something!" Razor tugged at the collar of his jerkin. "It's getting as hot as fire in here!"

"No. Wait!" Grey Cloak said. "I need more time. I feel a soft spot."

The rock walls of the tower glowed like coals in a forge.

"We can't wait any longer!" Tatiana said. "I'm disconnecting from Ugrad. I have no other choice."

"Hurry!" Tinison screamed. "I think my hair is catching fire!"

Crane grabbed Anya. "If I go, I want to go with you."

She picked him up by the waist and set him down by the thrones. "No, thank you."

"I only need a few more seconds," Grey Cloak said.

"We don't have a few more seconds. Take the helmet off. It's possessing you," Zora warned him.

Dyphestive yanked the helm off Grey Cloak's head. "No more."

"No!" Grey Cloak pleaded as he clutched at the helm.

Dyphestive held it tight.

Tatiana passed her hand over the pedestal. The image in the mural became blank, and the walls started to cool.

Crane let out a sigh and put his hands on his knees. "Look at me. My hands are shaking, and my clothing is soaked. I felt like a goose boiling in a kettle."

Grey Cloak squatted and shook his head. "I might have had him."

"Might isn't good enough. We almost died," Zanna said as she fanned her face. "Maybe next time."

"What about the tower in Ugrad?" Zora asked. "Is it still standing?"

Black Frost shut off his fire. The entire tower glowed like a hot blade in a blacksmith's kiln. Then the rocks cooled, and the bright-orange luster faded. The Wizard Watch had stood against the assault.

With a flick of his tail, Black Frost smashed through the brittle walls, revealing an empty level of rock and dust. He scraped his claws through it, picking away at the remains of his enemy. There were none.

He shoved the tower over. It toppled like a tree and hit

the ground in an explosion of dirt and debris. "And they said the Wizard Watch would never fall. They were wrong. That was easy." He stirred the rubble with his tail. "Look for any remains. Any item that might be of use. One tower is toppled, but there are still many to go. And once they fall, the enemies' plans will be doomed."

"We need to get the Apparatus of Ruune built and fast," Grey Cloak said. "Nath, how long will it take?"

He shrugged. "You'll have to ask your dwarven friend. I don't have any idea."

"Dyphestive, I'll leave it to you to handle the plans and get them to Rhonna. As for the dragons, I think it's time to return to Safe Haven."

"And what are you going to do?" Zora asked.

"I'm going to stay here and help keep an eye on Black Frost." He reached for the helmet. "And see what I can do to keep him from toppling any more towers. Because if he destroys them all..." He looked at Tatiana.

She finished, "I fear we're doomed."

13

IN THE FOUNTAIN level of the tower, Grey Cloak clasped hands with Dyphestive. "Farewell, brother. Tell Rhonna hello for me."

"I will, but I think you should come with us. Let the wizards manage the tower. You're one of us."

"I would, if my gut didn't tell me otherwise. The important thing is that we all reunite with one another. If the towers are lost, we shall meet in Safe Haven." He pulled a medallion from his pocket and handed it to Dyphestive. "Keep this so that we can find you if the need ever comes. Zora can find you."

"Say, what are we waiting for?" Crane asked. He sat in the front of his wagon with Zanna beside him. Shannon and Tinison rode in the back. "I haven't been to Dwarf

Skull in a long time. And I can't wait to meet this Princess Rhonna."

"Queen Rhonna." Dyphestive shook his head and said to Grey Cloak, "This is going to be a long ride, isn't it?"

"And bumpy. Are you sure you don't want to ride on dragons?"

"No, they'll be looking for that. Best we lie low." Dyphestive tapped Grey Cloak on the head with the Apparatus of Ruune's instructions. "See you soon, brother."

Grey Cloak nodded.

Dyphestive climbed into the back of the wagon. The wood creaked, and the wagon rocked.

Crane turned around and said, "Looks like Charro's got her work cut out for her today." He flicked the reins. "Yah!"

Zanna waved back at Grey Cloak. The bond that had been broken between mother and son was slowly being stitched back together. She'd done what she had to. They both had. They were much the same in that manner.

The stone door came down, and the rugged landscape of Crow Valley vanished, leaving Grey Cloak alone in the entrance chamber.

Anya and Cinder had departed for Safe Haven earlier with the other dragons, leaving Streak the only dragon behind.

"Are you all right, boss?" Streak asked. He had grown to nearly a grand-sized dragon, and he lay on his belly with his head inside the stone ring of the fountain, which had once been filled with cool and crystal-clear water.

Grey Cloak's fingers twitched. "Do you ever get the feeling you might not see someone again?" he asked as he joined his friend.

"No. Dragons don't think like that. We view everything as a potential next meal. So in that sense, we don't plan on seeing anything living again after we eat it." He licked his snout. "But I don't view you as a snack, or the others. Well, most of the time." He peered into the fountain. "But I sure could use some of the delicious fish that once filled this bowl to the rim. Ah, that silverfish was the most succulent morsel I'd ever eaten way back when I was a runt." He smacked his scaly lips. "I can still taste it when I burp. Say, when all this is over, let's go fishing. What do you say?"

"I can't wait." Grey Cloak placed both hands on the flat part of Streak's snout. "You've been a great friend. I never doubted for a moment that I picked right when I chose you."

"Yeah, you chose me because you didn't figure I'd grow big enough to ride on. Clever, but that backfired on you, didn't it?"

"So it did. But the looks on everyone's faces when I waltzed out with you that day was priceless."

Streak nudged him with his nose. "Yeah, well, I'm glad you picked me too. Now get up there with the others and find a way to save the world. I'm hungry."

Grey Cloak headed back up to the Chamber of Murals, where Tatiana, Gossamer, and Dalsay were working behind the Pedestal of Power. Zora was curled up in one of the pewter thrones, napping. Gorva lounged in the other throne while Razor leaned against it, humming.

Magnolia sat cross-legged, meditating behind the thrones.

Nath was nowhere to be seen.

The mural's image was that of the surrounding area, east of the Great River, closest to Littleton. Dirklen remained pacing outside.

"What's the story with him?" he asked Tatiana.

"He comes and goes, the same as he has been," Tatiana answered. "No doubt he's sending information to Black Frost."

"I believe he's the eyes on this tower while the armies rest their eyes on the others," Dalsay added. "All the towers are under siege except for the two farthest to the south—this one and the one in Sulter Slay. But they will arrive here soon enough. But which one will Black Frost hit next? And I mean him, not his armies."

Grey Cloak approached the mural. "If Black Frost is on the move, won't the temple be exposed? Can't we invade that spot and try to destroy his gateway to Nalzambor?"

"At best, only one of us could approach the temple," Gossamer replied as he lumbered down from the pedestal's dais. He held up the Ring of Teleportation. "It took me as far as the base of the temple, but I can only assume it is still under heavy guard. It would be one against an army of dragons. And I'm certain there would be other snares and traps to overcome."

"If any at all," Nath said as he ambled into the room. His long red-streaked hair hung down to his chest. He held a small wheel of cheese that was half-eaten. "I fear that Black Frost has drained all he needs of my world. I don't believe that genie can be put back into the bottle, so to speak."

"Genie?" Grey Cloak asked.

"A magic creature of myth believed to grant wishes." Nath clawed his fingers through his beard. "Very trouble-some. But the conundrum is that destroying his portal won't reverse the damage that has been done. It will suffo-cate my world. Black Frost must be destroyed, and his stolen power, in theory, should return to my world."

"Then why did Zanna and Olgstern Stronghair try to destroy it long ago?"

"Because Black Frost was not so strong then. Nalzambor could have survived the damage, but now, it is impossible." Nath patted Grey Cloak on the shoulder. "Your thoughts are brave and noble." He looked at Dirklen in the mural. "But I have a feeling you need to contend with him. He's trouble."

14

SULTER SLAY

THE WAGON RUMBLED and rocked over the dirt road, and the hot southern winds kicked up dust in their faces.

Shannon's eyes were squeezed shut, and she coughed from time to time.

Tinison lay down in the wagon bed. "This is insufferable. It's no wonder no one wants to live down here. It's nothing but dust and no rain. Ack! Another grain of sand. Just what my palate needed. Crane, I need something to drink."

Shannon kicked him. "Stop complaining. You're an embarrassment to the Honor Guard."

"What Honor Guard? I think we're the only ones left. Everyone else sold out."

"It was either that or have their heads cut off. We saw plenty of them roll from the executioners' block firsthand."

"No need to remind me. I had plenty of friends back there too. Good men and women, and we ran like cowards, only to wind up as human dust devils."

Shannon stiffened. "Don't say that. We fight on so that they didn't die for nothing." She kicked him again. "Halfling."

"Ow, that hurts," Tinison said.

"I take the sound of children squabbling as a good sign," Crane commented. "It means there is hope."

"Children?" Shannon asked with a raised brow.

"Trust me, darling. When you're as old as I am, everyone is a child." Crane winked at her. "Don't worry. These dust storms come and go. I've ridden through them a dozen times, if not a hundred. I always lose count after three. Not sure why."

Sitting in the front bench with Crane, Zanna turned around and said to Dyphestive, "Will you hand me my rucksack?"

Dyphestive swooped up a bag made of sackcloth. "This one?"

"That's it."

He gave it to her.

With a serious expression, Zanna rummaged through it and removed a blue velvet purse with golden strings pulled tight around the neck. She tossed it to Dyphestive, who caught it gently. "This is yours."

"Mine?" He gave it a curious look. "What is it?"

The hot winds suddenly died down.

"Finally," Tinison said as he rolled over to one side. "Well, open it up, Meat Skull. We'd love to see what you have in that dainty little purse."

Dyphestive unfastened the drawstrings and dumped the contents into his hand. A gorgeous square ruby rested in his palm. "I know this."

"That's one big jewel." Tinison reached for it. "Let me see."

"I don't think so." Dyphestive turned around to where the Iron Sword lay. It had an empty square spot in the cross guard, where the corners pointed north, south, east, and west. He snapped the ruby into the slot. "This was in the sword when I found it at Thannis. I became separated from the sword, only to find it again in Ice Vale but without the stone." He scratched the back of his head and gazed up at Zanna. "How did you do this?"

"I've spent a great deal of time acquiring items from Batram. He's a wily old goat."

"You can say that again," Crane added. "Did I ever tell you about the time—"

Zanna put a hand on the older man's shoulder. "Not now."

The gemstone glimmered with its own fire. Warmth spread from the double handle into the muscles of Dyphestive's arm. "What is the stone?"

"It's a blood ruby. Enchanted by my late husband, Jerrik Paydark. He and your father were friends. Your father forged the Iron Sword with his own two hands." She smiled. "He always said he built it for you, even before you were born. The blood ruby strengthened the metal. With it inserted, the blade is supposed to be unbreakable and can cut through anything."

"Lethal," Tinison said.

"It has other attributes," she continued. "But I can't comment on that. When Jerrik and Olgstern were together, they could become long-winded." Zanna glanced at Crane. "If you follow me."

"I'll take that as a compliment," Crane said. He handed her the reins. "And look who's doing all the talking now." He took out his pipe and tobacco pouch. "But you talk. I'll make some plumes."

Dyphestive tightened his grip on the handle with one hand and touched the stone with the other. "When I found the sword, the Goblin King had it, but there wasn't a stone. What happened?"

"When the time came to move against Black Frost, we knew our chances for success were slim. Olgstern didn't want the sword falling into the enemies' hands. He hoped it would one day find its way to you in case we failed. And it did. The Iron Sword, Reaver of Chaos, was destined to be yours."

A chill ran up Dyphestive's arm.

"Look at that. He's got goose bumps," Tinison said. He shivered. "Ooh, I do too."

"It's a gorgeous weapon," Shannon interjected. "Unlike any I've ever seen."

"But can it kill a dragon the size of a cliff?" Dyphestive grinned, set it aside, and covered it with a blanket. "I hope to find out."

They traveled in silence for the longest time until the wagon rolled to a stop.

Charro snorted and stomped her hooves.

"What's wrong. Why did she stop?" Zanna asked.

Crane huffed out a ring of smoke. "Because something is amiss."

Ahead, sand started spouting out of the earth. The ground heaved, and the wagon's wheels trembled. Monsters burst out of the earth.

15

CRANE'S PIPE fell out of his mouth.

Three sand monsters the likes of which no one had seen before erupted from the bowels of the wasteland and surrounded Talon. The size of grand dragons, they towered over the wagon, and they had bodies like scorpions but with dragon scales.

"Somebody tell me I'm dreaming." Tinison pulled his sword free. "Because those are the ugliest things I've ever seen."

"Those are desert scorpans," Zanna said. She drew her smaller blades and charged them with wizard fire. "I've heard of them but never seen one. Their stingers have poison. Watch out for them."

"I'll get us out of here!" Crane said. He grabbed his whip. "Back up, Charro. Back up."

The beautiful black mare snorted and began backing away.

The front scorpan scurried right at the horse and struck out with its tremendous black pincers. One of them swung around and clamped over Charro's neck.

"No!" Crane shouted.

The wild scorpan sheared Charro's head clean off. *Snip!*

Crane clutched his heart and sagged backward.

Zanna shoved him into the back of the wagon just as another pincer poked at him. She sank her sword into the claw, making green juices spit out. "Get under the wagon, Crane. Get under it now!"

Dyphestive snatched up the Iron Sword and jumped out of the wagon. "It's thunder time!" He charged the nearest monster and plowed his sword deep into its face, between its four sets of eyes. Green goo spit out all over him. He cocked the sword back and swung again, lopping off one of its two pincers at the wrist.

The hideous monsters' dark scales and spiny ridges glinted in the bright sunlight. The scorpans moved as one toward the greatest threat, Dyphestive.

"Watch out, Festive!" Zanna warned him.

He turned in time to see a stinger poised to poke a hole in his skull. It came down swiftly, but he caught it with his free hand below the bulbous base. Venom dripped out of the tip and over his hand, burning his skin like fire. "Aaargh!" He chopped through the appendage and flung it away then watched in horror as his skin was being consumed. "Thunderbolts! It burns everywhere."

Zanna leaped from the wagon and onto the back of the scorpan assaulting Dyphestive. She drove her burning blade into its back and started sawing.

Wings like a mosquito's unfolded from the scorpan's back and buzzed to life, and the monster took flight.

She jumped off and watched the ugly thing fly into the sky as goo dripped from its body. Some splattered on her head. "Ick!"

One scorpan still stood. Shannon and Tinison flanked it and attacked its rear legs.

"For the monarchy!" Tinison bellowed. With his wooly hair flying, he bull-rushed his stout frame into the scorpan's backside and hacked away.

The scorpan shifted around as quickly as a cat and slugged Tinison with the side of its pincer, knocking him flat.

Tinison rolled across the ground and popped up just in time to see its stinger coming down. "This is going to hurt," he said as he parried with both hands on his sword.

Shannon shouted, "No!" just as the stinger punched through Tinison's defenses and popped clean through his armor.

Tinison stiffened, and his head snapped back as he screamed. He hacked into the scorpan's tail one last time then said, "Long live the monarchy!" and died.

With the Iron Sword gripped in his one good hand, Dyphestive mowed through the desert scorpan, hacking it into bits and pieces.

Zanna and Shannon joined in the attack, shredding the monster into nothing but scales and sticky green goo.

The monster let out a dying shriek, spit blood, and finally collapsed, spasming until it twitched no more.

Shannon scurried to Tinison's side and cradled him in her lap. Tears streamed down her cheeks. "No, Tinison, you can't die!"

The scorpan's stinger had eaten the man from the inside out. His skin had already shrunk, and his eyes dissolved in their sockets.

Shannon wept.

Dyphestive knelt and cried with her.

Dirt covered Charro's body, leaving nothing left of her remains.

Tinison was given as much of a proper burial as their present conditions could provide.

Crane spoke on Tinison's behalf as well as Charro's. His soothing, rich words spoke about the exemplary and brave life Sergeant Tinison of the Monarchs' Honor Guard had lived.

The skin of Dyphestive's hand returned, but the pain came and went.

Crane insisted on not leaving his wagon, but they couldn't leave him behind, either, despite his assurances that he would be fine.

Dyphestive hitched himself to the wagon and took Charro's place. As sure-footed as a mountain goat, he pulled for mile after mile, league after league, not stopping once.

A sad-faced Shannon sat in the back of the wagon with Zanna while Crane had returned to his bench seat.

As the sun started to set, Crane said, "It's nearing the end of the day, Dyphestive. You can take some time to rest."

He shook his head. "I'm not tired. I'll walk through the night. All of you can rest."

"Be reasonable, Festive," Zanna said as she covered a sleeping Shannon with a blanket. "You need to save your strength in case we cross paths with more danger."

"Oh, I'm certain danger is coming, and when it does, I'll be ready."

16

THE WIZARD WATCH

MAGNOLIA TOOK a deep breath and watched her brother in the mural. She coiled a strand of her wavy hair around her finger. "I don't like the idea of killing Dirklen. He's my brother."

"A brother who tried to murder you," Razor reminded her as he donned a cloak and clasped the neck hook. "Not to mention the rest of us. I can still feel my guts leaking inside me." He fanned out his cape, which was dark blue and had a silver lining that shone like a moon. "And look at this ridiculous garb. How am I supposed to fight in this?"

"We aren't trying to fight," Grey Cloak said as he helped Zora fasten an identical cloak. "We'll use them to hide the Thunderstones, while he'll think we're using them for protection."

"The shield cloaks are designed for wizards," Tatiana

said as she prepared a tray of vials. "They help guard from physical harm. They'll significantly reduce your chances of dying quickly."

"Well, thank you, Tat." Razor shook his head. "Why didn't you give me one of these years ago?"

"At the time, they weren't mine to give, and you aren't a wizard."

Grey Cloak continued, "The goal is to strip Dirklen of the Stone of Transport. If we can achieve that, we'll have the full power of the Apparatus of Ruune." He eyed Nath. "Because we need them all, right?"

Nath nodded. "Judging by Black Frost's immense power, I think if we are to stand any chance, you will need them all. I don't see another way around it."

Razor flipped his cloak. "Well, I hope to fight him. Regardless of what happens, we owe him." He tucked his hand into his cloak and revealed the Thunderstone embedded into the armor on his chest. "This ought to square us up."

"The stone gives you powers but not the strength Black Frost imbued Dirklen with," Tatiana said. She gracefully moved toward all of them with a wooden tray of vials. "Drink this. It will enhance all of your abilities."

"You don't have to tell me twice." Razor picked out a tube-shaped vial with a bright-orange liquid that fizzled. "Bottoms up." He drank the contents, smacked his lips, and nodded. "I feel better already."

Grey Cloak, Zora, Razor, and Gorva each had a Thunderstone fastened to their chest. All of them drank, even Magnolia.

"It's hurtful that I have not been trusted with a stone," Magnolia said.

"No offense, but you aren't a member of Talon," Zora replied when she dropped her vial back into the tray. "You're the decoy, but you can earn your way today. If you can't convince him, and he tries to kill you, we'll protect your backside."

Magnolia returned a smile and asked, "Feeling spry, are we, little part elf?"

"Actually, I am," Zora responded.

Dirklen vanished from the mural, as he often did.

"The time to go is now," Dalsay said. "You need to be in the field before he returns."

"Everyone knows the plan, right?" Grey Cloak asked.

"Aye. We've rehearsed it a dozen times," Razor said. He scraped his swords out of their sheaths and spun them around. "Let's do this."

Grey Cloak moved toward the center and put his hand in the air. They all joined him in the same manner. "In the words of my brother, 'It's thunder time!'"

"Waaahooo!" Razor called.

Outside the tower, Grey Cloak, Gorva, Razor, and Magnolia waited near the spot where Dirklen had last been seen.

Streak circled beneath the clouds, and Zora was nowhere in sight.

Grey Cloak got itchy fingers. His cloak gave a subtle pulse. The air prickled, and Dirklen appeared twenty feet away from Magnolia.

"Well, well, well," Dirklen said with his sword resting on his shoulder. "Look who's returned for another whipping." His eyes flashed with fire. "This time, I won't hold back."

Magnolia stuck out her arms and pleaded, "Dirklen, wait! Hear me out one more time. I know you. You listen to reason, like Father."

"Like Father?" he cried. "Our father whom they killed?"

"Father died in battle with honor."

"Oh, well, like father, like daughter, so will you." Dirklen's gaze moved quickly from his sister to Grey Cloak, Razor, and Gorva. He glanced at the tower where the barrel of its defense system pointed at him. "I know you're up to something. I'm far from the fool you believe me to be." He looked at Grey Cloak. "And I noticed your dragon soaring in the air."

"Well, they do enjoy flying." Grey Cloak tapped the Rod of Weapons on the ground. "We're trying to resolve this peacefully. You know we need the stone to defeat Black

Frost. We can't do it without it. But if we have it, we can win. Join us, Dirklen. Do the right thing for once in your life."

"Right thing?" Dirklen snarled. "Who's to say that I'm wrong and you're right? I am right. Black Frost is right. The strongest are meant to rule, not the weak, such as you."

"Rule what, Dirklen?" Magnolia interjected. "A world in ruin? People who live in fear and terror? There is no joy in that." She moved closer to him, stepped on her cloak, and stumbled.

Dirklen snorted. "What are you wearing? You look like fool in that. All of you do." He flipped his sword around. "Is it a weapon you believe can destroy me? Nothing can destroy me."

She straightened her cloak and stood up. "No. But it will stop you from destroying us."

"No, sister. It won't. And I've had enough of this talk." His eyes heated, and he let loose his fire. He hit Magnolia as she covered herself in the cloak. The blast knocked her many yards backward. He laughed. "How'd that taste, sister?"

"Enough is enough!" Grey Cloak said. "Talon, take him down!"

17

Magnolia rose to one knee. The shield cloak radiated blue and shone like metal armor. She gave Grey Cloak a nod. "I'm fine."

Holding a pair of swords, Razor slowly advanced toward Dirklen.

Gorva moved behind Dirklen.

"Before you disappear like a coward," Razor said in his rugged voice, "why don't we all spin the steel against one another one more time."

"Three against one?" Dirklen scoffed. "I still heavily favor myself."

Grey Cloak retreated a bit. "I'll stay back."

"Yes, you do that. Probe for weakness, but it won't do you any good." Dirklen pivoted and fired rays of fire from his eyes into Gorva.

She stabbed her spear into the ground and vaulted over it. Flipping over in the air, she sailed above him and jabbed.

Dirklen sidestepped, and Gorva's spear pierced the ground where he'd been standing.

Razor snuck toward Dirklen and jabbed at him with both swords.

Clang! The Risker knocked both weapons aside and spun away. "Nice try, mortal, but you'll have to do far better than that to stop me."

"I'm not even warmed up." Razor caught Gorva moving in. "Let me have this. I can take him." He swung his swords around his body. "Time to find out whether you're all talk, Dirklen."

Dirklen's red-hot eyes cooled, and he drew a dagger. "There's nothing I like better than a two-fisted fight." He darted toward Razor.

Metal skipped against metal in a shower of mystical sparks.

They pushed against each other chest to chest. Dirklen, the taller of the two, leaned on Razor. "Fool, you are no match for me. I have the strength of a dragon."

"And I have the strength of something else." Razor kneed Dirklen in the groin. "Gumption and grit!"

Dirklen pitched forward, and Razor hit him in the back of his head with the pommel of his sword. The metal bashed hard against his skull. His opponent staggered, and

Razor flipped his blade end over end and chopped down in a lightning-quick stroke.

Dirklen grabbed Razor's arm. Through gritted teeth, he said, "No, you don't." Bolts of energy fired from his eyes, straight into Razor's chest. The blade master sailed backward, landed, and slid across the grass.

Gorva pounced. The head of her spear clipped the metal breastplate below Dirklen's ribs and drew blood.

"Gah!" He jumped back and fingered his bloody stomach. "No matter. It will heal." He sliced his sword in front of his face. "I don't know you so well. Gorva, isn't it? Daughter of Hogrim, the dead Sky Rider."

She spun her spear around her back and held it behind her, leaning forward. "I am my father's daughter, and as I recall, your father is dead too. Prepare to have your reunion first."

"This is laughable. Your spear is too clumsy a weapon to match my blades. But have at it, Gorva. I shall teach you a lesson in life and death that you can soon share with your father." He raced right at her.

She stabbed at his shoulder right before he dodged, and the blow knocked him off balance. She pierced his thigh, and he fell.

"Impossible. How did you do that?" He brought his sword up and climbed to his feet. "No one moves that fast."

Gorva kept her steady gaze on him. "It seems to me that you're slower than you think." She jabbed at him.

Dirklen blocked, and the spear slipped away from his parry and punched into his other thigh.

"No more!" he roared. Rays of light shot from his eyes.

Gorva ducked under them, took a swipe at his legs, and knocked him on his backside. Then she went for the kill.

Suddenly, Dirklen vanished and appeared behind her.

She flipped her spear around and stabbed backward.

He drifted back out of harm's reach. "How are you doing that? You anticipate my moves. Anticipate this!" He fired rays from his eyes, vanished, then did so again and again, each attack in a wink of time.

A flicker of energy clipped Gorva in the shoulder as she moved smoothly from the fifth attack. She spun to the ground, and her cloak opened fully, revealing the burning tangerine-colored Thunderstone of Sight.

Dirklen pulled back. "Ah, I see, you're using the Thunderstones against me. What does that allow you to do? See the future?"

Gorva got up. "I don't need magic to see your future. You are doomed."

Grey Cloak, Razor, and Magnolia joined Gorva, and they opened their cloaks, showing the stones. All four of them shone as brightly as the sun.

"This is your last chance to surrender, Dirklen. It's either that, or you can run away like a coward," Grey Cloak said.

Magnolia stretched out her hand. "Join us, brother. Please, do it for me."

Dirklen shook his head and sneered. "I don't think so, sister. You might think you have the advantage, but this fight is far from over. And I'm not running. I promise you, I'll return shortly." He vanished.

"Where did he go, Gorva?" Grey Cloak asked.

"I saw him move into the clouds." She looked up and narrowed her eyes.

Grey Cloak took a glimpse for himself.

Streak floated behind the pillowy field of white.

Out of nowhere, a thunder of dragons of all shapes and sizes burst through the clouds and descended like razor-sharp hail upon them.

Grey Cloak shouted, "Streak! Watch out!"

18

Dragons burst through the clouds and descended on him like a maelstrom of doom. Two grand dragons dropped right into his path. Fire spit from their mouths.

He rolled to one side, wings stretched out.

Riskers fired arrows from their saddles. Some of the missiles skipped off his scales but not all. One pierced the membrane of his wing.

Streak's tongue flicked out of his mouth. "You're going to pay for that! And not with cash either!" He made a smooth loop, flew upside down, twisted upright, snatched one of his human attackers from the saddle, and let the man drop. "Bye-bye!"

A grand dragon smashed into Streak's blind side. They locked claws, tails, and horns. He dug his talons deep into the dragon's flesh and tore hunks of scales from his body. The dragon let out a monstrous roar.

Streak clamped down on the attacker's throat with his jaws. He bit deep, hot blood gushing in his mouth, and let his flame out, searing the enemy's throat.

The hulking dragon spasmed and kicked once, then twice, launching his rider into the air.

Streak released the dragon, letting him plummet toward the earth. The rider fell alongside him but fired another arrow. It skipped off of Streak's skull right before man and dragon smashed into the ground.

"That was gutsy," Streaks commented. "Literally and no pun intended. Well, yeah, pun intended."

Then a ball of fire blasted into the side of his head.

He let out a roar and dove.

Dragons, led by Dirklen on the back of a grand who dwarfed all others, were attacking his friends on the ground. They swooped across the prairie and turned the grasses into flames.

Through the smoke and haze, Streak watched his friends scatter. He made a quick count of the group of dragons.

"Two down. Two dozen to go. Or is it a score? I don't know. I'm so bad with numbers." He spotted a pair of middling dragons without riders bearing down on Magnolia, who was sprinting across the field. "But I am good at flying."

He pumped his wings, picking up speed.

Magnolia ran like the wind, shifting directions and ducking under a lethal set of claws.

The pair of middlings grazed over her and turned.

Streak winked at Magnolia as he soared over her head. "I really hope she's on our side. Very pretty. A shame if she isn't. But evil sure can look beautiful."

The middling on the right finished his full turn, and his eyes widened when he saw Streak, who spewed a geyser of flame into the dragon's eyes and smacked into him, driving him into the ground. They thrashed over the grasslands, bigger against smaller. A moment later, the middling let out a dying croak and settled on the ground, with his flesh and scales in Streak's jaws.

Magnolia sent a charge of energy spitting out of her hand, cutting her attacker in two. One side of the beast crashed into one side of her, and the other half, the other.

"Whoa!" Streak landed beside her. "That was cool!"

She gave him a curious look. "Cool? Isn't hot more like it?"

He patted her with his wing. "Stick with me, and you'll catch on." He lowered himself. "Hop on."

Grey Cloak came out of nowhere and jumped on his back. "Sorry, Magnolia. You can catch the next flight." He eyed Dirklen, who was soaring overhead. "This trip is mine. Ride the sky, Streak! Ride the sky!"

"I think there's room for the both of us," Magnolia said.

But with a whoosh, they took off and left her in the grass.

"Where to, boss?" Streak asked. "Let me guess. The charming fellow with the bitter face?"

"None other, but our plan has gone awry," Grey Cloak said. "Didn't you see those dragons hiding in the sky?"

"Honestly, boss, it's as if they came from nowhere."

"How can that be?" Grey Cloak asked, more or less to himself. "Does Dirklen have that much command over his Thunderstone?"

"I don't know, but would it have killed you to give me one? You know how I like to wear something pretty."

"Next time, perhaps."

Streak bore down on Dirklen and his dragon, who were flying away. "That dragon is huge. Look at him move!"

"That's Waruum. We killed Dirklen's other dragon. I can only imagine he's bitter about that, but we'll kill this one too."

"Cold-blooded. I like it."

"But Waruum wasn't so massive the last time I saw him. Look at those horns, ridges, and scales."

Waruum was black with gold tortoiseshell-patterned scales. His horns radiated gold.

"If I were to guess, I'd say Black Frost gave him the touch too. Be careful."

"Careful is my middle name... not!"

They closed in on Dirklen, who twisted around in his saddle and gave an evil smirk.

Grey Cloak's skin prickled. "I don't like this."

Suddenly, Dirklen and Waruum vanished, as did all the other enemy dragons.

"Zooks! Where did they all go? Dirklen didn't even touch them."

The Cloak of Legends pulsed.

All the dragons appeared on the ground at once, trapping Gorva and Razor and unleashing dragon fire upon them.

From somewhere high in the sky, Grey Cloak heard Dirklen laugh, but he couldn't see him.

19

___

RAZOR TACKLED Gorva and drove her into the ground.

"What are you doing to me? Get off!"

"Covering you! We're about to be turned into a firepit!" he said.

The ring of dragons breathed all-consuming fire over both of them.

They cowered under their shield cloaks. The fabric hardened with a crystalized energy, absorbing the flames.

"It's working!" Razor said. Sweat built up on his face and dripped from his chin. "If we don't make it, I can't think of a better way to go than with you by my side, love."

"Don't get mushy now. We *are* going to make it."

The energy shield started to splinter and crackle.

"You'd better be right, or we'll be a pair of burnt biscuits soon enough." Razor's skin became as warm as toast and got even hotter. Dragon fire began to bleed through the shield cloak. "How about one more kiss before we go?" He made a kissing sound. "I'd love to taste those hot lips one last time."

Gorva rolled her eyes, but drops of sweat dripped from her nose. "Is that all you can think about in this moment of peril?"

"That's all I think about in any moment of peril."

The heat of the dragon fire pushed down on them like a great weight.

Razor's arm hair started to crinkle. "Razor blades! I'm burning! Auugh!"

"Stop crying. My hairs are burning too."

"I'm not crying." The stink of his flesh cooking made his nose crinkle. "But I will be when my skin turns as crispy as charred duck."

Gorva reached for his hand. "We'll make it. Hold on!"

They held tight to each other.

"You know, with all the dragons in my life, it never even occurred to me that I'd be cooked alive." He shrugged. "I never saw this coming." He kissed her knuckles. Grimacing, he said, "Gorva, it's been a pleasure."

"Yes, I know."

The flood of dragon fire came to an abrupt halt, and cooling wind whispered overhead.

Razor opened his eyes. "Are we dead? I'm chilly all of a sudden." He peeked through the hood of his cloak.

The dragons backed up, spread their wings, and flew away.

Razor pulled down his hood and stood up with Gorva. "What happened? They're leaving."

"Good," she said. The Stone of Sight glimmered on her chest. "I told you we would be fine."

Inside the tower, Tatiana took off the Helm of the Dragons, sagged against the pedestal, and moaned. "I did it. I sent the dragons away. But I don't have the strength left to control Dirklen. Working on the Pedestal of Power has exhausted me."

Gossamer put an arm around her waist and held her steady. "If needed, I can try."

"No, I need you to control the pedestal while I rest. We'll have to leave it to Grey Cloak to handle it." She eyed the mural. "Nath, you know the plan. Once Dirklen appears..."

Sitting on the throne, with his arms resting on the weapon controls, Nath replied in a scratchy voice, "I know. And I can't wait to blast him."

Grey Cloak and Streak watched the thunder of dragons disperse but saw no sign of Dirklen on land or in the sky. With the danger passing, they soared through the sky, doing their best to keep an eye out in all directions.

"Take us down, but don't land," Grey Cloak said.

"Aye, aye. Going down." Streak glided toward Magnolia, Razor, and Gorva and made a slow, sweeping circle, with the tip of his wing grazing the tall grass.

"Gorva, do you see anything?" Grey Cloak asked.

She shook her head. "I sense nothing."

"Well, stick to the plan. We've made it this far, but be ready for more surprises. Apparently, Dirklen isn't as foolish as we hoped he would be. Zooks! We were so close."

"My brother is no fool," Magnolia said as she made a slow turn and surveyed the sky. "He's cunning and cruel. I wouldn't be surprised one bit if he didn't have several more plans in mind. And if he was wise, he'd stay away, but I don't think he will."

"Look!" Razor pointed to the sky.

Dirklen and Waruum reappeared high above, twice the height of the tower level.

"Remember the plan," Grey Cloak reminded them. "Upward, Streak. Let's go say hello."

"There's nothing I like better than a fiery greeting." Streak flapped his wings, and they jetted into the sky. "Onward!"

Grey Cloak narrowed his eyes, and his mind raced.

He'd tried to anticipate Dirklen's every move, but the seasoned Risker had proved to be every bit as crafty as he could be. Grey Cloak touched the blue Thunderstone fastened to his chest. It controlled the elements, but he'd yet to use it. "I'm going to try something."

"You do that."

They closed in on Dirklen and faced off, hovering.

"You're losing, Dirklen," Grey Cloak said as the wind picked up. He noticed that Waruum wore a metal skullcap strapped over his face. A purplish gemstone burned brightly on the top. "But by the looks of it, you're prepared to lose with style. Nice jewelry, Waruum. Did you pick that up at Dark Mountain's finest jewelry shop?"

Waruum puffed out a plume of fire and gave a thunderous roar.

"Jest all you will, Grey Cloak. But that helmet you see will protect him from your control," Dirklen said. "And with another dose of power given to me by Black Frost, I'm more than prepared to finish all of you off once and for all." His eyes flared like shooting stars, and he fired.

20

SSTREAK TURNED AWAY but not quickly enough. Dirklen's energy ripped through the membrane of his wing. "Gah! That stung!" He turned tail and flew away.

Using the Stone of the Elements, Grey Cloak summoned a mighty wind.

It rocked Dirklen in his saddle, and he clung to the reins. "Nice try, fool! But a little wind never hurt anybody!"

Grey Cloak shouted, "How about this, Dirklen—me versus you. Let's see who the best dragon rider is."

"I've no time for your childish games." Waruum soared after Streak. "How about dragon against dragon?"

"Fine by me," Streak said. He turned in midair and faced off against the far bigger Waruum. "Let's see what you got, ugly."

Waruum let out a roar. His chest heaved, and the scales of his breastplate flexed out and brightened. A blast of red-hot fire came out of his mouth.

Streak spit out his own fire.

The flames impacted and curled in the sky. It wasn't long before Waruum's fire began to swallow Streak's.

Grey Cloak leaned down and said into Streak's earhole, "Listen to me. I can aid you, but move so that their backs are to the tower and between us."

Streak shifted his direction, as if he were trying to escape.

"Here goes!" Grey Cloak placed his hand on the Stone of Elements. Mystical energy surged through his body. He focused on Streak's flame and made it stronger than ever before.

Streak's funnel of flame grew, shoving Waruum's fire back toward his mouth.

"No!" Dirklen said, his cheeks red with rage. "You are stronger, Waruum! Stronger than ever! Destroy them!"

Waruum's fire shoved back, and the surge pushed into the very fiber of Grey Cloak's body.

Zooks! He's impossibly strong!

Streak beat his wings with feverish intensity but still started to glide backward. Even with Grey Cloak's help, his dragon breath began to sputter, but he did get Dirklen and Waruum lined up between himself and the tower.

"Hang on, Streak!"

The tower's cannon was lined up with Dirklen and Waruum. Grey Cloak couldn't help but smirk.

Dirklen caught his expression and looked uncertain.

Wah-Boom! A green torpedo of energy shot out of the tower's cannon. It struck Waruum right between the wings and under Dirklen's saddle.

"Bullseye!" Grey Cloak shouted.

Dirklen fell from his saddle. His eyes were closed.

Wings beating, Waruum managed a staggered flight, but his breath went out.

"I'm going after Dirklen. Can you handle Waruum?" Grey Cloak asked.

"You know it!" Streak replied.

Grey Cloak dove out of the saddle and aimed toward Dirklen.

Please don't wake up!

A moment before Dirklen splattered on the ground, he vanished.

"Horseshoes!" Grey Cloak shouted. The ground rushed up to meet him, so he flipped upright, and the Cloak of Legends billowed out, slowing his fall.

Dirklen reappeared several dozen yards away, staggering across the grass and rubbing his head.

"There!" Grey Cloak said to his comrades. "After him." He glanced up and saw Streak bearing down on Waruum. "He'll be fine. He'd better be."

Another torpedo of magic blasted a disoriented Waruum in the head. He let out an angry roar and turned toward the tower's weapons.

Streak landed on Waruum's back, sank his teeth into the massive dragon's wing, and ripped the flesh from the muscles and scales. When he jumped away, he was still holding the wing in his mouth.

Waruum's anguished roar could be heard for leagues. He plunged toward the land, one wing beating furiously, making him spin in a circle.

Streak spit the wing out of his mouth. "I hope he lands on Dirklen."

The beast dragon fell with a resounding thud.

"Nope. Missed by a mile." Streak dove and summoned his fire. "Time to finish the job, 'cause someone is serving Waruum for dinner tonight."

As four of the members of Talon closed in on Dirklen, he blinked from one spot to another in an erratic pattern.

Grey Cloak commanded the grass to coil over Dirklen's feet and hold him fast, but Dirklen ripped out of them as if they were dry noodles and vanished again. He reappeared behind Gorva and shot his eye beams into her back, flattening her. Parts of his armor were broken off. Other pieces hung on from leather straps. The tower's torpedo had done some damage.

"It's over, brother," Magnolia said as she spun around, looking for where he might land next. "Surrender."

"Don't plead with him anymore," Razor said as he helped Gorva back to her feet. "He's had his chance. It's time to ruin him."

Grey Cloak's energy dropped. The potion Tatiana had served them was wearing off. They'd given Dirklen their best shot, but he was still standing.

Dirklen appeared beside Grey Cloak and punched him across the jaw. He snaked his head back just enough to avoid the full impact of the devastating blow, but he spun around and executed a leg sweep.

Dirklen lost his footing and fell.

Grey Cloak, Razor, Gorva, and Magnolia piled on top of him, holding, clawing, punching, and grasping at the Stone of Transport with everything they had.

Dirklen let out a hyena-like cackle. "Your efforts are so feeble that they don't even tickle." He started to stand, like an iron tower being raised. He grabbed Gorva's hand that was trying to clutch the stone and bent it backward. *Snap!*

Then Dirklen let out a pulse of wizard fire that sent them all sprawling across the prairie.

They landed hard, and the strength seeped from their bones.

With his hands on his hips, Dirklen glowered at them. "Victory is mine!"

21

Streak lowered his horns and bore down on Dirklen.

"This is laughable." A shot from Dirklen's eyes hit the dragon and sent him rolling backward.

He dusted off his hands. "That should finish it. Time to make their inevitable deaths permanent this time."

Everyone but Zora was down. Using the Scarf of Shadows, she'd waited for her moment to strike. She possessed the yellow Stone of Power. Grey Cloak had planted a decoy on Magnolia.

She balled up her fist, reached deep, and summoned her courage. Grey Cloak started to rise as she moved right in Dirklen's path.

The man's hard stare bored a hole through her as if she didn't exist. Feeling the Thunderstone's fountain of might in her fingertips, she latched onto Dirklen the moment he reached for his sword. "Surprise."

"What in the blazes?"

With the strength of a giant coursing through her veins, Zora reappeared, clamped her hand over the Stone of Transport, and crushed through the metal that held it fast.

Dirklen seized her arm and tried to pull it free. "You dare? You foolish little part-elf worm!" His burning eyes met her gaze. "I'll put a hole through your head!"

Zora clung to his body, ducking her head aside, and stuck the Ring of Mist in his face.

The tiny flower petals opened, and a fine white mist sprayed into his mouth.

He coughed and spit, blinking wildly. "What trick is this? Is this supposed to make me sleepy? Fool!" He headbutted her.

Pain exploded in her face unlike any sensation she'd experienced before. But the Stone of Power gave her strength. It burned like the sun and fed her. Zora set her jaw and headbutted him in the nose. Cartilage broke, and blood began to flow.

"Witch, get off of me!" He clutched at her throat. "I'll take you on a ride you'll never forget!" he said, and they both disappeared.

Moving from place to place, they appeared in the sky, on top of the tower, back on the ground, and in the sky again, wrestling for possession of the stone. She'd never had such strength before. But if she lost, Dirklen would win, and all of them would be dead.

Using his metal gauntlet, he beat her savagely. Her blood rained down on the earth, and her grip on the stone started to loosen. He pried her hand free with one hand and punched her in the face with the other.

When she'd grabbed the stone, she should have yanked it off. But she'd hesitated. It gave Dirklen time to recover. He was starting to win—again.

No. I can't let them down. I won't *let them down. I'm sick of this.*

Taking one pop in the face after the other, she said, "Dirklen, you might win, but I want you to know something."

"What's that, dead woman?"

"I hate you!" She launched her Thunderstone-powered knee into his groin and watched his eyes bulge. With a fierce yank, she ripped the stone free of his chest, then she descended toward the ground.

I got it! She looked down. *But who's got me? How do I work this thing?*

Falling like a stone, she waved her arms frantically. "Help!"

Zora's bowels twisted. She spun then was suddenly lying on the floor in the tower, at Tatiana's feet. The Stone of Transport rolled from her fingers. "Did I do it?"

Tatiana knelt beside her. "You did it." She looked at the mural. "But Dirklen isn't finished yet."

No sooner had Dirklen crashed to the ground than he was on his feet again and surrounded by his enemies. His broken armor hung from his limbs, and his chest was heaving. Nostrils flaring, he said, "I don't need the stone to kill all of you. I have more than enough power to finish you off. I'm not even tired."

"Maybe you aren't tired, but we're tired of you," Grey Cloak replied. He was exhausted and aching inside and out. The use of the stone had drained him. He amped up the fire in the Rod of Weapons. "And I'm more than ready to dance you straight into the grave, where you belong."

"Once again, laughable." Dirklen's eyes charged up, and he drew his blades. "You move like old people."

Razor crept behind Dirklen. "Stand still."

Dirklen froze in place as the whites of his beady eyes expanded.

"And shut your yapper." Razor cut Dirklen's head off in a swift, clean strike.

The head rolled across the ground, but the body stood its ground.

Razor opened up his cloak and showed the Stone of

Command's burning pink light. "Huh. Pink looks good on me."

Streak scurried over and gobbled up Dirklen's head. He swallowed and let out a smoky burp. "He's not going to be shooting any of us with those crazy eyeballs anymore." He burped once more. "But I already feel some heartburn coming on. Does anyone have a giant flask of Pepto?"

Dirklen's body finally fell.

The fire in the tip of the Rod of Weapons cooled. Grey Cloak took a knee, smiled, and said, "I told you I'd think of something. Did any of you ever have a doubt?"

Streak wagged his twin tails, and with a smile as charming as a crocodile's, he said, "I never doubted you for a second."

22

Back inside the Time Mural chamber, Grey Cloak approached Zora, who was sitting on the stairs below the throne, holding a damp rag against her swollen jaw. Dirklen's metal gauntlets had lacerated her cheek and cut her deeply above the eye.

Grey Cloak handed her a fresh damp rag. "At least you didn't lose any teeth."

Peering at him through a puffy eye, she said, "No, but several are loose, and I don't think I can grow them back if they fall out, like Dyphestive did." She sighed, wincing. "I should be dead. He beat me like a drum. I'm not made for that."

"None of us are, but the Thunderstones kept us together. That and Tatiana's potion." He stretched out his arms and put one around her waist. "I think I could sleep for a week."

Zora leaned on his shoulder. "Me too."

"Your bravery is astonishing. I should have gone through that. Not you."

She shook her head. "No, it was a sound plan, much to my surprise. But it would have gone more smoothly if I hadn't hesitated. I had the stone in my palm, but my delay nearly cost all of us our lives."

"But it didn't. You beat him." He gave her hip a little squeeze. "You deserve a parade."

"Ha ha," she said wearily. "I appreciate the thought, but I'd rather have a nap."

Nath moved beside them, sat down by Zora, and said in a wheezy voice, "That was an impressive plan. I have to say I enjoyed watching it unfold. Heh-heh. I wish I'd been wiser in my younger days. Would have saved me quite a few headaches."

Grey Cloak leaned forward. "Nath, are you well? You don't sound it."

Nath had aged noticeably since Grey Cloak crossed paths with him in a gnoll's holding cell near Farhook. Most of the red hair in his long gray-and-white locks was gone. The flicker of gold in his eyes had almost all been washed out by brown. Even the vibrant pep in his voice had lost most of its luster.

Nath gave a dry cough and said, "Don't write me off yet.

Though I think I might have passed, if not for the recovery of the Thunderstones." He gazed at the ring of five stones, which hovered in the air near the pedestal. "They give my spirit strength." He squeezed Zora's knee. "Grey Cloak is right. You've shown a great deal of inner strength. Work with it."

Zora nodded and said, "Thank you." Then she looked up and gasped.

An image of Black Frost had appeared in the mural. He was storming right toward them, with an army of dragons flying above him.

Grey Cloak stood. "Where is this?"

"The tower south of Loose Boot," Tatiana replied.

Black Frost's eyes brightened like huge cauldrons of burning blue fire. The spiny ridges on his shoulders started to glow, and the creases between his chest scales burned brightly. A waterfall of blue fire cascaded from his mouth.

The air inside the chamber heated.

"Don't fight it, Tatiana," Dalsay warned her. "That tower is lost. Let it go. Break the connection."

"We can't let him destroy them all." Tatiana's fingers glowed over the stones.

Everyone stood.

Razor fanned himself with his hand. "It's getting hot in here, Tat! I don't want to be cooked twice in one day."

"No!" Tatiana said, wild-eyed. "Bring me the Helm of the Dragons. I can stop him!"

"There is no choice!" Dalsay said. He moved to the pedestal. "Look at me, my wife! The longer you fight it, the more of our power is drained. Let down those defenses. Cut it loose, before he takes this tower down with that."

Tatiana threw her hands up and shrieked. The chamber dimmed, and the air cooled. She placed her hands on the rim of the pedestal. Sweat dripped from her nose. "You are right, husband." She took a deep breath and peered at the blank slate wall in the archway. "Sadly, that makes two towers he has destroyed in two days."

"How many are left?" Razor asked.

"Four."

Razor wiped the sweat from his brow with his thumb. "Are you telling me we only have four days to stop that monster?"

"Yes," Grey Cloak said. "Unless we find a way to slow him down or the Apparatus of Ruune is completed."

"How do you suppose we slow down that monster? It would be easier to stop the wind," Razor stated. "We had a hard enough time with Dirklen. That evil bas—"

Gorva nudged him.

Magnolia had just reentered the chamber. He gave her an uneasy glance. She'd kept her distance from the group after the battle.

"It's fine," Magnolia said. "My brother is dead, but he had it coming, and I've come to terms with it." She touched the scar on her cheek. "Though a part of me is shredded inside. I still loved him. I have a thought, however."

"What's that?" Grey Cloak asked.

Magnolia strolled deeper into the room and stood before the levitating ring of Thunderstones. "We know that Dirklen is dead. Black Frost does not. Perhaps we can fool him."

"Are you suggesting we do something similar to what I did with Zanna and Datris?" Gossamer asked. "Have someone else take on another disguise?"

Grey Cloak grinned. "Magnolia, I like the way you think. Can it be done?"

Gossamer nodded. "I don't see why not."

23

SULTER SLAY

CRANE WIPED his sweaty face with a rag and took a swig of water. "I've been to Dwarf Skull before, but I don't remember it being this far away. And I don't recall the sun being so hot either. I might have to take my jerkin off."

Zanna was seated beside him on the wagon's bench. "It's probably best that you don't. Your pasty skin would burn to a crisp."

"Pasty?"

She laughed. "Only jesting. How are you coming along, Festive?"

Dyphestive towed the wagon into a dry creek bed and up the other side. His bare back, packed with bulging muscle and bronzed by the sun, flexed and heaved. "Never better."

Shannon moved up from the bed of the wagon and

squeezed between Zanna and Crane. When she saw Dyphestive, her eyebrows rose.

"I see someone got her rest in," Zanna said as she stroked Shannon's hair.

Shannon covered her mouth, yawning, but her eyes were glued on Dyphestive's muscles. "How long can he keep pulling the wagon?"

"He hasn't slowed down yet." Crane fanned himself. "I've been wanting him to go faster, since the air died down, but I thought that might be rude."

"It *would* be rude."

"Well, you're obviously enjoying his efforts," Zanna quipped.

"Huh?" Shannon tore her eyes away from Dyphestive's back. "I'm not going to pretend I don't have admiration of his, well, physique."

Crane blanched. "What? You're attracted to that? Look at all those lumps all over him. He looks like his skin's going to burst." He patted his belly. "You need a portly man, like me. My hugs are soft, but his will hurt."

Shannon gave a devilish grin. "I bet they would."

"Shame, shame," Zanna admonished her. "But I can't say I blame you."

Crane shook his head and rolled his eyes. "Women."

They traveled another league and spotted great hills in the distance.

Dyphestive stopped and turned.

Crane threw him a towel. "I know what you're thinking. Is there a road through those hills? There is. We can navigate it, but it's a climb."

Dyphestive wiped his face. "I'll be fine. How about some water?"

Hopping out of the wagon, Shannon said, "I'll bring it." She hurried over to him with a waterskin. "I don't know how you do it."

"I got used to pulling plows when I worked on Rhonna's farm." He took a knee and hung the towel over his neck then poured some water over his neck and shoulders and drank. "Thanks."

"You're welcome."

He handed her the waterskin and looked at Crane. "How much farther is Dwarf Skull once we cross these hills?"

"At this rate, I'd say it will take one more day. We've made good time. Not as good as Charro, rest her dear soul, but you've done well."

Zanna slid out of the wagon and stretched her arms and legs, twisting and bending over. She rubbed her backside. "My own saddle is sore. I suppose I could walk from here." She eyed the rugged hills. "Are there dangers out there?"

"The dwarves always controlled the land between the Split Rivers. I'm surprised we haven't crossed paths with them. But if there are any about, they'll be watching."

"Or something else will be," Dyphestive said. "We're sitting targets out here in the open, and there really isn't a way to sneak."

"Unless we travel at night," Zanna suggested.

Dyphestive picked up the wagon's tow bar. "No, we've come this far, and I'd say they've seen us by now, if they're there. Might as well go say hello and hope for the best."

"Hold on," Shannon said. She pushed Dyphestive aside and grabbed the tow bar. "I want to try."

"You're welcome to." He stepped aside.

Shannon fit herself into the harness, pulled the straps over her chest, and dug her feet in, leaning forward. Her attractive face filled with strain. She puffed, and the wagon inched forward. Planting one foot at a time, she kept going.

"You have a strong back and legs," Dyphestive commented as he walked beside her. "Well done."

"Look at that," Crane said. His mouth hung open. "She's pulling it like a mule. A pretty mule but a mule nonetheless."

Shannon pulled the wagon across the rough terrain for the better part of a mile. Her cheeks were flushed, and every step took a mighty effort. Finally, she fell to her knees, gasping. "Monarchs of mercy!" She gave Dyphestive an incredulous look. "How do you do it so effortlessly?'"

He shrugged. "I guess I have a knack for it."

She eased out of the harness and dusted her knees off. "Better you than me. But I'm walking from here."

Dyphestive pulled the wagon to the base of the hills, took a narrow trail, and started the upward climb.

Zanna and Shannon walked behind the wagon.

"You're a natural. Can you pull a wagon like that?" Shannon asked.

"Festive inherited his great strength from his father, Olgstern Stronghair. It's his primary gift. So don't be ashamed of yourself. You're clearly as strong a woman as any."

"I don't know about that. I'm strong but not like an orc, by any means."

"Don't underestimate yourself. I've known plenty of orcen women who couldn't pull that wagon. Warriors too."

The wagon stopped, and they moved to the front.

A huge pile of rubble blocked the passage halfway to the top.

Dyphestive removed the harness and said, "This isn't good. I can move the big stones, but there are so many little ones."

Lighting his pipe, Crane said, "The sun is setting. These hills will be as black as coal soon. It's the perfect place for an ambush." He blew out smoke. "What do you want to do?"

Dyphestive moved to the rubble. "Dig."

24

"Dyphestive, you need to rest," Zanna urged him. "I know your strength is boundless, but your mind can become weary." She patted a spot on the ground beside her. "Join me."

He heaved the boulder on his shoulder away. He'd been moving the pile for over an hour and made little more than a dent in it.

"We might have to walk," he said.

"Listen, everyone. I told you, the wagon and I will be fine. You can go ahead without me and send someone back," Crane said in a huff of pipe smoke. "I practically live in this thing, you know. It wouldn't be the first time."

"How will you defend yourself?" Shannon asked.

Crane casually flipped a hand. "The same way I always do. I'll talk my way out of trouble." He tipped his head toward the top of the hill. "Dyphestive, take the road to the top. See if you can see the lights of Dwarf Skull from there."

"Not a bad idea." He stood.

"I'll join you," Shannon said. "I've never seen Dwarf Skull before. I'd like to glimpse it with you for the very first time."

"Come along."

"I'll make sure Crane is safe while the two of you go scouting." Zanna pulled her knees to her chest. "But I think these hills are abandoned. We should have come across some dwarven soldiers by now. Wouldn't you think so, Crane?"

"Agreed."

Dyphestive climbed over the barricade of rubble and started up the trail.

Shannon kept pace with him, her hand brushing his from time to time.

"You'll like Rhonna. She's tough like Tinison. Well, tougher. As tough as anyone I know," he said.

"Even you?"

"Ha. Far tougher than me. She drove Grey Cloak out of his skull. A laborious taskmaster, she was."

"She sounds like a lot of fun."

"Rhonna certainly is, if not having fun, considered fun."

Shannon laughed. "I like your dry wit. I find it soothing."

"Uh, thank you."

She grabbed his hand. "Does that make you uncomfortable?"

"No, not at all."

Shannon stopped him, pulled him closer, rose on tiptoe, and kissed him.

He felt both of their hearts pounding.

She broke it off and said, "I hope you don't mind."

"No, uh, not at all. It was nice." He held her hands, leaned down, and kissed her again.

Under the blanket of warm darkness and a star-filled sky, they hugged and kissed for the longest time.

A scuffle caught Dyphestive's ear, and the hairs on his neck rose. He shoved Shannon to the ground and said, "Look out!"

Something hit him on the side of his head. He staggered down to one knee, turned around, and faced his attacker, a towering brute with a club held high. He swept the attacker's legs from under him.

"Urgh!" the brute yelled as he fell on his back.

Dyphestive pounced on the bigger foe. They thrashed across the road in a tangled knot of muscular limbs. He struggled to match the brute's raw strength. A hard fist crashed into the side of his head, but he punched back. *Whack! Crack! Thump!*

"You're a strong one, but you've underestimated me!" He drove a boot into the tremendous man's belly.

"Oof!" The attacker doubled over, swatted at Dyphestive, and ripped into the meat of his arm.

In the darkness, it was difficult to make out what sort of muscle-bound race his attacker was.

What is he? An ogre? A big orc? He's powerful and even stronger than me.

Dyphestive cocked back and hit the attacker in the jaw.

A fierce punch walloped Dyphestive in the gut. "Oof!"

They wrestled over the road. The attacker's small horns dug into Dyphestive's face. He locked his fingers around Dyphestive's neck and squeezed like a python.

"Urk!" Dyphestive pulled his knees up, planted his feet in the attacker's chest, and thrust with all his might. "Eeryah!"

The monstrous man struck a wall of boulders piled up near the road. He slowly started to rise from the pile.

Dyphestive charged. "Stay down, lunk!"

The creature threw his arms up and yelled, "Dyphestive! Stop! It is I, Tiny!"

Skidding to a stop, he said, "Tiny? Show yourself in the light."

Tiny did, and Dyphestive got his first full look at the cyclops he'd befriended so very long ago. The giant of a man, though small by cyclops standards, had the same warm expression on his face. "It *is* you!" He embraced the bigger man. "Why did you attack me?"

"Sorry, but it's survival of the fittest out here." Tiny

picked Dyphestive up and squeezed until his back cracked. "It's a great joy to see you, brother! What are you doing here?"

"Traveling to Dwarf Skull again."

Tiny set him down. He turned and looked at Shannon, who had her sword out. "I won't hurt you, lady. I'm a friend."

"You're a big friend." She sheathed her sword and moved closer. "Whoa, you're a cyclops. I don't mean to stare, but I've never seen one before. I wasn't even sure they existed."

Tiny said in his deep voice, "Now you know." He clamped his huge paw on Dyphestive's shoulder. "You've gotten much stronger. And so fierce. I'm proud of you."

"Thanks. And your speech is much clearer."

"I've been practicing."

"So, where's Chopper?" Dyphestive asked of the gnome who'd befriended him. "Tell me he's alive."

"Alive and well." Tiny waved them onward. "Come. He'll be eager to see you."

25

CHOPPER JUMPED for joy the moment he laid eyes on Dyphestive. The small sand gnome leaped into his arms and squeezed his neck. In a scratchy but peppy voice, he said, "I can't believe my impish eyes! Look at you! And you've grown some too." He hopped down and did a little dance. His bare feet kicked up dust, and his tattered clothing would have fallen off if not for his suspenders. "'Tis a good sign! 'Tis a good sign, it is!"

"It's good to see you again, too, Chopper." Dyphestive stepped closer to the campfire. "These are my friends Crane, Zanna, and Shannon. We lost a comrade, Tinison, along the way."

"A shame," Chopper said as he rubbed his furry beard. "What took him?"

"Scorpans," Zanna said.

"Ugh! Hate scorpans. Taste bad too. No good in them at all."

Chopper scurried over to a log near Zanna and Shannon and jumped onto it. His foxlike facial features crinkled. "Women!" he said. "I have not seen a woman in years. And this pair is gorgeous." He looked at Dyphestive. "Where did you get them?"

"Excuse me," Shannon said.

Crane let out a jolly chuckle. "Take no offense, Shannon. He's a sand gnome. They live in isolation, and there aren't any women among them."

"Not that we don't like their company." Chopper winked at Zanna and nudged her with his elbow. "But our ways are harsh. Women don't take a liking to our nomadic ways. But I must admit, I've never seen a star in the sky as pretty as the two of you."

"Ah." Zanna patted him on the head. "You're a cute little man too."

Chopper jumped up and clicked his heels. "Tee-hee! She touched me." He jumped away and raced around the small campfire. "My cheeks are on fire. I believe I'm blushing."

"He excites easily," Tiny said. He picked up some large flat stones that would take four ordinary men to carry and set them down by the fire. "Please, sit."

"Yes, yes." Chopper nodded eagerly. "Let's talk." He dashed away and vanished into a hole in the ground then reappeared moments later with a hand-carved pipe in his hand. It was made of beast horn, like a ram, and curled. He stuffed tobacco into it and lit it with a stick from the campfire. "Dyphestive, what brings you here?"

"I would ask you the same. You moved, it appears. Why here?"

Chopper passed his fire stick over to Crane, who joined him in smoking, and said, "Ah, yes, smoke with me, friend. I hate to smoke alone. Tiny won't join me."

"Smoking stinky," Tiny said.

Crane shrugged. "You think he complains—you should hear my ex-wives."

Chopper's face lit up. "How many wives have you had?"

Crane looked at Zanna and Shannon. "Including them, thirteen or so."

"Egad! And you are still living and breathing?"

"We aren't married to him," Shannon stated. "He's jesting."

"Oh." Chopper scratched his head. "Tee-hee." He poked his pipe out and said, "Funny. We don't get many laughs these days. As for us, well, the plains became too dangerous to live in." He made a bitter face. "Ugly dragons cross the skies. Destroy everything. It's easier to hide in the hills. We need cover."

"What about the dwarves? I thought they patrolled and mined hills like this," Crane said as he huffed out a ring of smoke. "I haven't seen any sign of the beards."

"And you won't either. Most of the dwarves are dead. Those dragons have wiped them out. Overtaken Dwarf Skull. It is little more than a prison—a tomb for the dwarves—now." Chopper sighed. "I'm no lover of dwarves, but I pity them. They never saw it coming."

"I thought the southern lands were safe," Dyphestive said. "What about Queen Rhonna? Is she alive?"

Chopper shrugged. "I can't say. If she's not dead, she's a prisoner." He sighed out a breath of smoke. "I'd rather be dead than a prisoner. So, what is your business in Dwarf Skull? I take it it's more than a friendly visit."

Dyphestive shared a glance with his comrades. Zanna gave him a terse nod.

"We have a way to destroy Black Frost. We need the dwarves to help us build the contraption that will do it."

"Contraption?" Chopper rubbed his jaw. "Now you're speaking my kind of language. What sort of contraption is this? You have a wagon? Is it a wagon?"

"No, that's my wagon," Crane said. "The contraption he speaks of is more complicated."

Chopper's fingers fidgeted at his sides, and he said, "I'd be honored to see what it is."

"Me too," Tiny grunted. "I've never seen a *con... trap... shun.*"

"Well said, my friend."

Tiny sat up and beamed.

Dyphestive fetched the plans for the Apparatus of Ruune and rolled them out near the fire.

"Here," Crane said. He flipped a coin, which glowed like a moon. It landed on the parchment.

Chopper snatched it up. "Too bright. Too bright. We can't risk the attention. A low campfire is one matter, but those sky serpents would zero in on this." He tucked the coin into his torn trousers. "But I thank you for it." He got down on all fours and scoured the plans. "This is fascinating. Indeed. Never imagined such a thing. And big. Very big. Bigger than your wagon. Rich in complexity." His dirty finger ran over the lettering. "I've spent time with dwarves. Understand their intricacies. This is without a doubt dwarven engineering."

"Can you help?"

Chopper shook his head. "I fear not. I was very young during my time abroad, meeting the people, and I cannot help you with this. Though I wish I could. However, there is a matter I *can* help you with."

"What's that?" Dyphestive asked.

"I can get you into Dwarf Skull undetected. But getting back out without being seen? That's a risk you'll have to take."

Zanna poked Chopper in the ribs. "You get us in, little man, and we'll get us out."

Chopper cackled. "Tee-hee. She touched me again."

26

THE NEXT DAY, Chopper led Dyphestive, Zanna, and Shannon toward Dwarf Skull, leaving Tiny and Crane back in the hills with the wagon. Sticking to the ravines that snaked across the dry landscape, they moved all day long and into the night. Finally, they spotted Dwarf Skull the lesser part of a league away.

Dyphestive pulled out a spyglass and stretched it to its full length. "Impressive."

Dwarf Skull was a fortified stone structure with octagonal walls. It appeared to be its own tiny mountain against the black hills. The outer walls were over thirty feet high and completely vertical. Torchlight winked between the battlements, and high defense towers were between each wall and in the corners.

"May I look?" Shannon asked.

He handed her the spyglass, but his eyes didn't leave the walls, where dragons were perched like gargoyles. Including the ones patrolling in the sky, there must have been several scores of them.

Shannon shook her head. "I guess we won't be going in from the top, will we?"

Chopper shook his head. "The tunnel is tight. I don't think you big-boned people will fit. Not a chance Dyphestive will make it. But Zanna, I believe you will make it."

"Whoa," Dyphestive said. "You and she can't go in there alone."

"Me?" Chopper touched his furry chest. "I'm only taking her so far. I won't go in myself, unless I have to. I'm a bit squirrelfish when it comes to danger. Can't believe I've made it this far. But for the cause, I build my courage."

"I'll be fine," Zanna said. "You know this is more my cup of tea. Besides..." She patted her own satchel. "I'm well-equipped for about anything."

Dyphestive handed her the plans and said to Chopper, "Do you think there's anyone she can trust inside?"

Chopper scratched his fuzzy cheek. "Funny thing about dwarves. They don't bend for anyone. They'll die first. I'd surmise that's why so many have been slaughtered and other forces brought in. But not all. Many have escaped, deeper south, I believe. Probably women and children. But other family members, if I were to venture a guess, are being held hostage in order to get cooperation. So if you see a dwarf, aye, I believe they will assist you. The issue will be moving through the stronghold undetected." He shrugged. "But what do I know? I'm only guessing."

He gave Zanna a serious look. "Stick to the plan. Find Rhonna, show her the instructions, and see if she can help. Then get out of there until we figure out what else we need."

Zanna nodded. "I'll be back soon. Lead the way, Chopper."

Digging into the side of a small ravine like a prairie dog, Chopper cleared the way to the mouth of a corroded metal grate. "An ancient drainage system runs from Dwarf Skull, replaced long ago. I think even the dwarves have forgotten about it." He tapped a finger to his skull. "But I remember."

"How old are you?"

"Sand gnomes live a long time and me more so than most." With an inquisitive expression, he said, "I might even be the oldest, but who knows." He started to worm his body down into the pipe.

She grabbed him by the foot and pulled him back. "And why would you know about these drains? After all, you're a gnome, not a dwarf."

"Dwarf Skull was not solely populated by dwarves long ago. Did they build it? Yes, but in a time when the Split

Rivers thrived with fish and the land was fertile from one side of Sulter Slay to the other. Always green. Always aplenty." He winked at her. "Don't you trust me?"

"No." She shoved him back into the pipe and climbed inside.

Chopper hadn't lied. Dyphestive wouldn't have fit in the tunnel, and Shannon, with her armor, was too big-boned. On her hands and knees, Zanna crawled after Chopper, her head scraping against the top.

It became a long, agonizing journey, and she fought to keep up with the little gnome, who was less than half her size.

As good as Zanna was at keeping track of where she was, in the pitch-black, she lost perspective. She kept pace with Chopper by listening to his scuffles and cheerful murmuring.

"Ew." She grabbed his leg and hauled him back. "What is that smell? It's awful."

"It wasn't me." He sniffed. "Ah, that is rather foul. You'll have to forgive me, but I'm used to Tiny being around. Believe me when I say his flatulence will cause one to leave all other smells unnoticed." He started to crawl away.

She held him fast. "You're taking me into the sewer tunnels, aren't you?"

Chopper held up the glowing metal coin that he'd taken from Crane. "It's the last place they'll think to look, eh?"

"I'm starting to think that's the reason you won't go any farther, not because you're scared."

"You know, for a such a pretty lady, you are very, very smart as well." He loosened his foot from her grip. "Come on, now. The sooner you get through it, the better."

She shook her head and followed. "So this is what I get for staying svelte all these years. I need to be more like Dyphestive and eat more."

27

"This is as far as I go," Chopper said. The tunnel opened to an abyss of sewage. His nose crinkled. "Egad, even Tiny would find this offensive. That must be centuries of waste brewing down there."

Zanna shielded her nose in the crook of her arm. They'd moved deeper than she'd imagined, and all she could see was the abyss and a pitch-black ceiling above her. "Let me see that coin."

"Certainly." He handed it to her. "You can keep it. I don't need it to return."

She held the coin overhead. The bright light penetrated the darkness, revealing the other side of the abyss. Wastewater poured from drains in the opposite wall, into the huge pool of sludge. "Don't tell me I have to go through those tunnels."

Chopper shrugged. "Not all of them leak. Some are used less than others."

"How deep are we?"

"About a couple hundred feet."

She pointed. "What's up there?"

Tilting his head over his shoulder, he replied, "Most likely solid rock. No other way to go but that way." He indicated the other side. "Sorry, but I know you can do it. Should I wait?"

"No. Go back and let everyone know I made it this far. If I run into trouble, keep an eye out for my signal."

"What sort of signal?"

"You'll know it when you see it." She tousled his hair. "Thanks, Chopper. You've been a good guide."

"Tee-hee." He scurried back into the pipe and sang, "She touched me."

Zanna put the coin of light in her mouth and started to climb the walls of the abyss. She found good purchase on the rocks and moved at a steady pace, crawling like a spider toward the oozing drains on the other side.

The effort wouldn't have been so bad if not for the offensive smell wafting into her nostrils and piercing her brain.

I should have brought Zora. She'd have been perfect for this. Ah, who am I to say such a thing? There is no one better than me. Ew! Once I get out of this, I'll have to wash myself inside and out somehow.

She made it to the other side and peeked into one of the drain holes. When a rush of liquid caught her ear, she jerked her head out of the way.

"Uck!" she said through clenched teeth. The sound was drowned out by the sewage splashing into the abyss. "Nasty. Only a gnome would lead me down here."

Zanna continued crawling along the wall, checking out the drains, until she found a dried-up pipe. Her nose crinkled as she sniffed.

This will have to be the one.

She wormed her way into the pipe, her neck hairs tingling. Then she eased back and peered down into the burbling muck of the abyss.

A mass of mud with a man's torso and sludge-like arms rose, and the stench worsened. The monster moaned.

Her stomach turned. *I'm not waiting to see what that is.*

Crawling on her knees and elbows, she scrambled into the pipe.

A loud moan followed her.

Then something coiled around her ankle and jerked her backward.

The coin dropped from her mouth. "Gack!"

A strong tendril started dragging her back down the pipe, and she kicked at it.

Another slimy tentacle snaked into the pipe and struck at her feet. It squirmed around like a snake. She kicked it again.

The hairlike fibers of the tendril stuck to her boot. In the wink of an eye, it circled her other ankle and pulled her out of the pipe.

"No!" Her fingernails dug into the muck. She flipped over to her belly, clawing desperately.

At the lip of the pipe, she found a grip and held on with all her might.

The sludge monster moaned again.

Zanna glanced down. It moved beneath her with a huge mouth gaping. More tendrils crawled out of its mouth and reached for her body.

She'd made a mistake and underestimated the massive monster. *Think, Zanna. You can't die like this.*

She stared down at the ugly beast. "Let's see how tough you really are."

Zanna summoned her wizard fire. It rose like an inferno and spread throughout her body. She shimmered orange from head to toe.

"Eat this!" She sent a wave of energy that shot out of her like wildfire. It passed through the tendrils like mystic flames.

The monster's mouth erupted into flames. Its haunting moan became a howl.

She gave it another blast of wizard fire, and it again exploded in the sludge monster's mouth.

The top of the monster's head burst apart, the tentacles released her ankles, and it sank back into the stinky depths.

"Whew!" Zanna crawled back into the pipe and caught her breath. "I hope nobody heard that."

She resumed her trek, grabbing the coin of light. "I guess we'll know soon enough."

Two Black Guard soldiers exited their bathroom stalls at the same time.

One asked the other, "What did you eat last night?"

The man glared at his accuser. "Wasn't me."

They both peered back into their stalls.

The accused man said, "Must have been the dragons."

"Ha, you always blame the dragons."

28

WIZARD WATCH

GOSSAMER'S TRANSFORMATION WAS COMPLETE. He had become an exact image of Dirklen and was even wearing Dirklen's battered armor. He shifted, adjusting the shoulder plates. "I don't know how warriors wear all this metal. There isn't a single area that's comfortable."

"I always thought all that armor was for halflings anyway," Razor said as he adjusted the breastplate's straps. "Not to mention it takes far too long to put on and take off. You have to live in it if you always want to be ready. No, thanks."

Gorva helped Gossamer slip one of the metal gauntlets on. "Don't listen to him. You'll get used to it. But with any fortune, you won't have to use it for very long."

He nodded. "I hope so."

Grey Cloak gave Gossamer a once-over. "Eerie how

much you look like him. I don't notice a difference. Quite a powerful spell."

"That, it is." Tatiana approached with a black leather satchel in one hand and the Star of Light in the other. She hung the satchel over Gossamer's shoulder. "You've been face-to-face with Black Frost before. Are you certain you can fool him again?"

"I can't be certain of anything, but I'll try. If I didn't have faith in all of you, I wouldn't."

Tatiana took out the teleportation ring that she and Gossamer had used. "This will take you there and bring you back. That satchel contains the decoy Thunderstones. My Star of Light will give them power, hopefully enough to fool Black Frost." She hugged him. "You are brave, my dearest friend."

Gossamer nodded. "I learned it from you."

"So," Grey Cloak said, "do you believe you can lead him to the tower north of Dark Mountain?"

Gossamer adjusted the satchel's strap and put the pink Star of Light inside. "It's not the most convincing story, but there is logic to it. I can only imagine he wanted to save that tower for last, since it's so close to Dark Mountain."

"If we force him back, that will buy a few days, maybe longer." Grey Cloak offered his hand. "Dragon speed to you, Gossamer."

"And you as well."

To everyone's surprise, Magnolia gave Gossamer a hug.

"I know this might seem strange, but I never got a chance to tell my brother goodbye. Not in a proper manner, that is." She broke off the hug, and with a tear in her eye, she caressed Gossamer's cheeks. "I love you and miss you, brother." Then she kissed his cheek and walked out of the chamber.

"That was bizarre," Razor commented.

Gorva shook her head.

"What? It was."

"It's time," Gossamer said. "Farewell, all. I hope to see you soon." He squeezed his fist and vanished.

"I have to hand it to the black-and-white one. He has some stones." Razor picked up a bottle of port. "What's the next move, fearless leader?"

"Now that we have the Thunderstones, I believe it would be wise to take everyone to Safe Haven. Aside from the mages." He moved toward the pedestal and grabbed the emerald Stone of Transport. He looked at Nath, who had his head resting on his fist and was leaning on the throne. "Ahem... is this difficult to master?"

Nath opened his eyes. "They follow your thoughts. The more you use it, the more comfortable you will become. It's no different from the stone you used before. Whoever possesses it is one with it."

Grey Cloak gave an approving nod, walked over to Zora, and took her by the wrist. "What do you say to a quick trip to Safe Haven?"

"With you in charge? I think I'd rather take my chances with Tatiana."

"I don't think so." He closed his eyes and envisioned the vault in Safe Haven, and when he opened them again, Anya's sword was pointed at his throat. "Surprise."

Anya's cheeks were flushed. She sheathed her sword and said, "Jumping dragons! You need to send out a warning before you do that."

Zora shivered. Her face turned pale. "I don't think I'll ever become used to that feeling. And my tummy had only settled after Dirklen. Now it's inside out again." She let go of Grey Cloak's hand. "Please don't take me anywhere else."

Grey Cloak smirked. "I'm not promising anything."

He disappeared and reappeared between Razor and Gorva then put his arms around their waists. "I think I'm getting used to this. Ready to go?"

Razor said, "Uh—"

"I'll take that as a yes." He took them to the vault and returned again.

"Zooks! That is exhilarating. Nath, I suppose you're next. Can you handle the trip?"

Nath groaned and got up from his throne. "At my age, I've seen and done everything." He ambled down the short flight of steps. "Believe me—nothing is going to surprise me."

Tatiana offered Grey Cloak a black satchel like the one she'd given Gossamer. "The stones are all inside." She reached into it and furrowed her bow. "Wait a minute. I think I gave Gossamer the wrong satchel."

"*What?*"

Tatiana gave a devious smile. "Fooled you."

Grey Cloak's jaw dropped.

"Look at him. He's at a loss for words. How delightful," she said.

"Well played, Tatiana. Well played. If there is one moment I'll remember with you, it's this one." He looked about for Magnolia. "I suppose I can return for her next. Be sure to round her up." He waved at Dalsay.

Dalsay gave him a nod.

Grey Cloak locked arms with Nath. "Oh. Tell Streak I'll come back for him too. Shame on me, almost forgetting my dragon." He winked, and they were gone.

29

DWARF SKULL

Zanna emerged from the drainage pipe into a deteriorating stable. In a bed of rotten hay, she stood and dusted off her clothes, sniffing herself.

I don't suppose I smell any worse than anyone else.

She bent over and rubbed her ankles. They had bloody rings around them, and they itched and burned.

Should have known the sewers would be alive.

The decrepit stable was nothing but a bed of undisturbed straw and dirt. The rafters were filled with cobwebs and bird nests. Bright little insects crawled along the posts.

Zanna moved out of the stable and into the barn. As she studied the architecture, she noticed that the layout was more similar to a barracks than a barn. Stalls were filled with bunk beds made for three and four people. The one she'd crawled through appeared to have been a washroom at one time, but it had been abandoned, for some reason.

Perhaps the dwarven soldiers who lived here fled or were killed.

If the dwarves had been killed, their families fled, and a host of Black Guards took over, there would be a lot of abandoned places.

She moved quickly through the dimness to the end of the barn, where it opened up into the streets.

Dwarf Skull was a fortress and a city all in one. The buildings were mighty, erect structures made of large rectangular stones cut to perfection. They weren't all dark gray, either, but many vibrant colors. Intricate, heavy-duty metal frames lined the doors and made magnificent archways and gateways through the streets.

Zanna crouched in the shadows and waited. On the building tops were the heads and horns of dragons facing outward.

Black Guard soldiers sauntered through the streets in small groups, talking and joking casually.

Dwarf Skull was a conquered city, dead in dwarf and spirit. A foreign invader had taken over.

Sticking to the shadows, Zanna followed some of the soldiers wandering the streets. Using the cover of night, she eavesdropped on their conversation.

"One must hand it to the dwarves," the tallest soldier in the group of five said. "They make a fine ale!"

"Hear! Hear!" the smallest man agreed.

"Quit smooching up, PeeWee. We're off duty. You can be yourself," the tall man said.

"Anything you wish, Commander," PeeWee said. "No more smooching up."

The commander sighed. "Why did the Riskers make you—a snot-nosed whelp—my charge? Why?" He slung his arms over the shoulders of two of his other men. "I don't care for bootlickers." He squeezed one soldier close to him and took a slug of ale from a tankard. "But this dark ale numbs my ears. Ah, it's empty." He stopped. "PeeWee!"

"Yes, Commander?"

The commander shoved the tankard into the little man's chest and nearly pushed him over. "Go back to the alehouse, fetch a small barrel, and bring it to the barracks. The night's not over yet!"

PeeWee held his trousers up with one hand and saluted. "Right away, Commander!" Then he scuttled back down the street.

Zanna crept into a slot between the buildings.

Perfect.

The group of soldiers teetered back down the street with the commander muttering, "I bet he can't heft it on his shoulder. He'll probably roll it, the little runt. Pah! I say we get him drunk and feed him to the dragons. Who'd miss him?"

Chuckles erupted.

Zanna tapped her finger on her chin.

What a wonderful idea. Thank you, Commander.

PeeWee came back down the street several minutes later with a small barrel of ale cradled in his arms. His knees wobbled, and he huffed and puffed all the way.

"I can do it," he said. "I'm strong enough." He made it one more block and teetered toward the buildings where Zanna waited in the shadows. He lowered the barrel to the edge of the road and wiped the sweat from his brow.

Zanna crept behind him and placed the edge of her dagger against his neck. She whispered in his ear, "Hello, PeeWee. Tonight is your special night."

He stiffened and gulped. His Adam's apple rolled under her blade, causing a nick.

"There will be more blood where that came from, if you so much as utter a word. Now, roll that barrel back into the alley with me."

He squatted and complied.

They faced off in the sanctuary of the shadows, and she kept her blade poised against his throat. She eyed the tankard in his trembling hand and said, "Fill it up."

PeeWee blinked several times then slowly descended to one knee. He pulled the cork out of the barrel, tilted it over, and poured.

The dwarven ale sloshed out, spilling over the tankard and onto the street.

He gave her a fearful look.

"It's fine. Keep pouring."

PeeWee wasn't such a bad-looking fellow. His big, round ears stuck out from his helmet. He had kind eyes but a weak chin. He gave a meager smile when he topped the tankard off.

"Excellent. Now, drink. Drink it all."

30

___

PEE WEE BELCHED SO LOUDLY that it echoed from one end of the alley to the other.

Zanna flinched then peered down the street and waited.

The streets remained empty. She poked PeeWee with her dagger and whispered, "Don't do that again. Understand?"

He hiccupped and said, "I'm sorry. I couldn't help it. The commander doesn't usually let me drink his ale." He sagged back against the wall. "Are you going to kill me?"

"Probably, but if you do as I ask, I might let you live."

Cradling the tankard in both hands, he drank until it was empty. "I don't think I can drink any more. So bitter." He rubbed his protruding belly. "I'm not used to this." He covered his mouth and burped again. "Sorry."

Zanna squatted, lifted his chin, and looked him dead in the eye. "I'm going to ask you a few questions, and I need you to answer them truthfully. Understand?"

He nodded.

"Where is Rhonna, the queen of the dwarves?"

"Oh, that's an easy one. In the hold. Lots of dwarves are in the hold. It holds many." He giggled. "Get it?" He frowned. "Sorry, no—*hic*—pun intended."

"Where is the hold?"

He pointed across his body. "South quadrant. Yellow banners, black bars. Dwarves put signs on everything. Durable ones. We spent time taking some of them down, but it took too long, and we stopped. Dwarves are difficult."

Zanna nodded.

"Are they under heavy guard?"

PeeWee shrugged. "Depends on what you consider heavy. The dwarves made their dungeons difficult to escape. It's perfect for their captivity. Dwarf-proof vaults."

"I see. Drink up."

He groaned and poured another. "Commander Edmund is going to be very upset that I drank his ale. Hates me enough as it is."

"You don't seem well-suited for the Black Guard."

"No, of course not. My uncle Fitzgerald is a Risker, my father is dead, and I don't know what happened to my mother. Uncle Fitzgerald said I needed to be stout—a better man, but I hate it. Wish I knew where my mum was or who she was. I bet she was nice." He looked up at Zanna. "Pretty, too, like you." He tilted his head. "You don't seem like an assassin."

Zanna raised an eyebrow. "Don't be mistaken. I've slain many."

"Black Guard?"

"Perhaps."

"Good." He drank deeply from the tankard. "Are you going to make me drink myself to death?"

"No, but when you wake up tomorrow, you're going to wish you were dead." She sheathed her dagger. "PeeWee, I need you to do one more thing."

He was drifting off and fighting to keep his eyelids open. "What?"

"I need you to take off your clothes."

"Really?" He smiled. "I'd be happy to." He puckered his lips. "But wouldn't you rather kiss me first?"

"That's not why I need your clothes. Save yourself. The right lady will come along one day."

PeeWee started to strip off his tunic but passed out first.

"Great." She dragged him deeper into the alley, stripped him down to his undergarments, and donned his armor. His slight build meant his suit fit her well. She donned the helmet. "Not bad." She rolled PeeWee onto his belly and against the wall then hid the barrel of ale with him. "Thank you, PeeWee. You couldn't have come along at a better time."

Staying in the narrow passages, Zanna traversed from the northern end of Dwarf Skull to the southern. As PeeWee had explained, finding the south quadrant wasn't difficult. The yellow-and-black banners hanging in the streets were easily spied too. A pair of them hung over an iron door that led into a jailhouse.

She snuck through the door and spotted a snoring Black Guard sitting on a chair with his helmet down over his face and his legs propped up on the desk. Behind him was a big door made of solid steel with a drop bar sealing it shut.

Hmmm...

The bar looked heavy, but the hinges were oiled, and the steel wheel to lift it appeared fully operational. She grabbed the wheel and twisted it counterclockwise. With the metal scraping against the door, the locking bar lifted.

The jailer snorted, rubbed his jaw, and lifted his helm. "What are you doing?"

"Shift change," she said, being careful to keep her helmet pulled down to her eyebrows and speak in a low voice, like a man. She certainly smelled like one.

He narrowed his eyes. "When did you start? I don't know you. Who sent you?"

Zanna gambled. "I'm part of the reinforcements that have been assigned to Dwarf Skull. Commander Fitzgerald wanted me to become familiar with the hold. I'm being assigned here. Didn't want to wake you."

"Fitzgerald, huh? Thinks he rules everything. Almost as bad as those Riskers." He dropped his feet to the floor. "But you're a fool. If you go in, a dwarf might waddle out."

"I didn't think that was possible."

He opened a deep desk drawer and withdrew a ring of intricate keys. They rattled as he wiggled them. "No, they won't get out without these. Took us forever to figure out what key went to which cell. But we did. Or I did, rather. Lucky me, the head jailer. What an honor." He rubbed the grizzly hairs on his jaw. "Say, what's your name, fella?"

"Morton."

"Morton. Heh, that's a funny name." He fanned his nose. "Whew. What did you do? Ride in a wagon of manure on yer trip?"

"Something like that."

"Move aside, Smelly. They call me Tatum." He opened the door. "Go on in. Take a look. The dwarves don't say a word. Fine prisoners. They won't harass you. Solemn, almost like a tomb. We take a few to a guillotine every day. Have to thin the herd. But tomorrow is the big day. Ought to break their spirits."

"Why's that?"

"That's the day Queen Rhonna dies."

31

THE HOLD WAS the cleanest dungeon Zanna had ever seen. The steel bars that caged the dwarves were polished. The walls were dry, and no foul smells lingered. If anything stank, she did.

A dwarf with a braided brown beard down to his knees was sweeping the floor with a handmade broom. Neither he nor any of the rest met eyes with Zanna.

She walked down the aisle, peering into the cells. The bars were two-inch-thick steel, and the locks had metal plates that covered the keyholes.

Every cell was the same, ten feet by ten feet. Several dwarves were in each one. Many cells were crammed full, and the dwarves sat or slept on one another.

The dwarven men all had beards. Some were braided,

and others were short and fuzzy. They were chestnut brown, bloodred, gray, and even as white as snow. Some dwarves' noses were big and hooked, but a few were like large buttons. Many had bushy eyebrows that stretched out beyond their faces. Others were neatly trimmed.

Among the hundreds of faces, Zanna saw no sign of Rhonna or any dwarf who wasn't bearded.

She came to an intersection and got her first eyeful of how large the hold was.

Great dragons!

A grid of cells lined the aisles. Some of them were only five feet by five feet, and only a dwarf or two lived in them. Others were larger, almost twice the size of the ten-by-ten cells. There were hundreds of them.

I should have asked Tatum where Queen Rhonna was. But I didn't want to draw suspicion.

She noted the ancient dwarven lettering above every cell. Though it was an older form of text, she could make it out.

One hundred twenty-three. Anvils, there're at least five hundred in this nest. And thousands of dwarves. Rhonna, Rhonna, where could you be?

She tried to catch the eyes of the four dwarves in one of the cells. "Listen, I'm here to help Queen Rhonna. Can you tell me what cell she's in?"

All four of them turned their backs.

"Fine." Zanna walked down the aisle again. "Rhonna. Can someone help me find Rhonna?" she asked quietly.

Not a single dwarf responded.

She pushed her face against the bars of another cell and called to a gang of dwarves within, "Do you know Queen Rhonna is slated to die tomorrow? I'm here to help. You have to believe me! Will somebody talk to me? Ugh!"

Zanna picked up the pace, determined to search each and every cell. "All I have to do is leave and come back with the cell number. But I don't want to do that, because I might be compromised. Please, for the Lords of the Air, will someone talk to me?"

"Why should we trust you?" a man with a soothing voice asked.

Zanna stopped, backed up, and looked into a ten-by-ten cell, where a lone man sat covered in his hood and cloak. "You're not a dwarf."

"You're very observant. Not all are dwarven in these depths. Tell me—who are you? Why do you seek the queen?"

"My name is Zanna Paydark. I need Rhonna's help, and she needs mine. We all do."

He stood and dropped his hood, revealing his orcen face. He had hard features but kind eyes as well as a full beard but no moustache. He approached her and wrapped his fingers around the bars. "Zanna Paydark is dead."

"No, I've been a statue. A very long story." She narrowed her eyes. "You're Lythlenion, aren't you?"

His eyes widened. "Yes. How did you know that?"

"Grey Cloak and Dyphestive have told me all about you and Rhonna. It might do you well to know that I'm Grey Cloak's mother."

Lythlenion studied her. "Yes, I see the resemblance. Are they with you?" he asked excitedly.

"Dyphestive is nearby. Outside the walls." She opened her satchel.

"How did you get in here?"

"The ancient sewers."

Lythlenion's nose crinkled. "Makes sense."

She unrolled the instructions for the Apparatus of Ruune. "This is a weapon we can build to destroy Black Frost, but only a dwarf can build it. I need to show this to her and find out if it can be done."

He held his chin and studied the map. "A fascinating contraption, but I can't read the lettering at all. Very, well, complicated."

"It's an urgent matter. Black Frost is destroying the Wizard Watch towers one by one. Once those are gone, there is little hope of stopping him." She rolled up the scroll. "I need Rhonna. We have to figure out a way to get her out tonight. She's being sent to the block tomorrow."

"Then I suppose we don't have much time." Lythlenion glanced into the darkness of his cell. "Do we, Rhonna?"

A blanket by the wall moved. Rhonna, with an expression as tough as nails, rose and draped the blanket like a coronation cape over her shoulders. She walked over, nodded at Lythlenion, and locked eyes with Zanna. "Let's take a look at those plans."

32

SOUTH OF LOOSE BOOT

DISGUISED AS DIRKLEN, Gossamer arrived near the remains of the Wizard Watch Black Frost had recently destroyed. Some of the rubble still glowed as hot as lava. The terrain was charred to a crisp, and small fires burned all around. Smoke moved over the valley, blanketing the Black Guard, who were breaking down their camp and preparing to march.

Everything was as he'd expected—worse even. Then he spotted Black Frost sitting among the hills, his snout turned south.

Gossamer's stomach knotted. *South is the last place I want him to go.*

He marched toward the great dragon, ignoring the soldiers' salutes and brushing by anyone who stepped into his path, the same as Dirklen would. When he came across the tip of Black Frost's tail, he could feel the heat coming from it. He stepped around and gazed up at the dragon who stood taller than hills.

This is it. Time to put on a life-or-death performance with the fate of all mankind at stake. I am Dirklen!

Gossamer moved before Black Frost, waving his arms and sweating from the heat of the dragon's scales. "Oh, Glorious One! It is I! Your servant Dirklen!"

Black Frost leaned down. His blue eyes were blazing with fire, which began to cool.

"Dirklen! Come up to me!"

Using his sorcery, he levitated to Black Frost's eye level. "I am here, Great One! I hold the power from their treachery." He extended the satchel with the decoy Thunderstones. "I defeated them but lost Waruum in the process. Though I have victory, I'm not without disappointment. A few still remain in the tower, and I'm working once again with my sister to root them out."

Black Frost snorted.

Gossamer continued, "My Lord, Magnolia has revealed to me their last desperate plan. They will use their remaining resources to attack the portal in your temple from the Wizard Watch northeast of Dark Mountain. I assume you want to spare that one for the future, but they believe there is a clear and present danger there. Would it be wise to dismantle that tower as well before they try one last desperate attack?"

"You say Magnolia informed you of these matters? How can that be? She is a traitor."

"She tried to sway me, but I swayed her when I defeated her and Talon." Gossamer turned on the bravado. "If you could have seen how I dispatched them." He clenched his fist. "It was a hard-fought battle, but with my strength enhanced by you, I was unstoppable."

Black Frost nodded. "You prevailed, my child. You have proven yourself. What do you feel I should do?"

"I am honored that you would solicit my opinion, but I trust in your wisdom." Gossamer remembered that Dirklen was brash and never humble. "But if it were me, I'd wipe out every tower from top to bottom. Who needs those wizards when you have all the power the world will ever need?"

Steam sprayed from Black Frost's nose, and he turned his gaze southward. His wings stirred. "There is little left in Nalzambor that I have not taken. Yes, it is possible that a danger still exists." He bared his tremendous teeth. "Even a gnat can cause a giant to stumble. Dirklen, I will heed your information. Send word to Dark Mountain. See to it that the tower is placed under siege." He closed his eyes. "Now I rest for the journey ahead. As my energies muster, I will contemplate the tower's destruction. Dismissed."

Gossamer bowed. "As you wish, Master of all Dragons and Conqueror of Worlds." He floated to the ground and headed back toward the camp. Cradling the satchel with his trembling hands, he wandered through the smoke.

I did it. He believed me. The world will be spared for a few days more.

He didn't dare a backward glance and marched on like he owned the camp.

And he didn't even want to see the Thunderstones. Intriguing.

Now he rests. Perhaps after taking a tower, he is weak. His powers aren't at their fullest. That might be the best time to strike. Hmmm. It all went so well, but why do I feel like spiders are crawling all over my back? I don't like easy. It's never been so. Why would it be now?

As the day went on, the Black Guard troops gathered in rows and ranks a thousand men deep. A score of Riskers circled in the sky and led the march south. Others remained behind with their magnificent leader.

Gossamer waited.

Black Frost didn't move until dawn of the next day. He opened up his eyes, flexed his wings, and turned north. He found Gossamer and said, "Ride with me."

"As you wish, Grand One!" Gossamer levitated and seated himself between the great scales of the dragon's neck.

They rose into the sky on wings that stirred the wind like a thunderstorm and didn't stop until they arrived in the north and landed a few leagues away from the tower nearest Dark Mountain.

Gossamer secretly pumped his fist in victory. *Yes!*

33

THE TOUGH-LOOKING dwarven woman ran her pudgy fingers over the plans, which lay on the cell floor. "We can build it." She cocked her head and leaned closer. "Where'd you say you found these plans?"

"Nalzambor," Zanna answered. "How long do you think it will take, Rhonna?"

"How long? Hard to say. The more dwarven hands I have, the better. I need at least five of my best engineers." Rhonna eyeballed the plans one more time then rolled them up. "My question to you is: How long do we have?"

"A week, possibly less."

Lythlenion cleared his throat. "Excuse me. That isn't a lot of time, considering we're still prisoners in the hold. Wasn't getting yourself in and out difficult enough? How will you manage a handful of dwarves?"

"And an orc." Rhonna handed Zanna the plans through the bars. "If I go, you go. And I imagine this elf didn't come in here without a plan."

"I was to find you and see if it can be done." Zanna folded the plans and tucked them in the satchel. "I would report back to Dyphestive and give him the layout. But the mission has changed, since they plan to kill you tomorrow. We need to get you out of here tonight."

Rhonna crossed her arms. "I'm ready when you are."

Zanna laughed. "Yes, well, I'm trying to think of something."

"You are Grey Cloak's mother. That's for certain," Rhonna said. "Back on the farm in Havenstock, I used to ask him how he'd get his chores done before the day ended, and he always said, 'I'll think of something.' It drove me crazy."

"Did he get them finished?"

"Next to never. Oh, but I made him pay for it." Rhonna managed a slight smile. "So, how are the boys doing?"

"You'd be proud. Thanks to them, Gapoli is still intact."

"Huh. In an odd way, I'm not surprised." Rhonna looked up at Lythlenion. "Got anything to add, old friend?"

"No, I'm as ready to depart from this snake pit as you are. But I have to admit I don't have the imagination to foresee how it can be done," he replied, a bit shamefaced.

Zanna poked him through the bars and said, "Leave that to me. We're going to need a distraction, but first, let me try something." She produced a ring of jingling keys from the satchel. "These are Crane's. He says they'll open any lock."

Rhonna arched an eyebrow, and with her arms folded across her chest, she said, "If they open these locks, I'm an ogre's behind."

Zanna stuck the first key into the hole and twisted it but was met with resistance. "Not that one." She tried one key after the other until she'd tried them all. "Hmm. It appears you're right."

"These locks are proofed against magic, unlike ordinary doors. Only the jailer's ring of keys will open them." Rhonna leaned against the bars. "Get those keys, and we can move out. All of us."

"What do you mean by all of us?" she asked.

"My kin are ready to fight. I say let them out, and we can swamp the Black Guard. How does that sound for a distraction?"

"I like it. But there are the Riskers to contend with." Zanna put the keys away. "Are there any other secret passages that lead out of this city?"

"Plenty."

Zanna nodded. "You've given me something to work with. Don't go anywhere." She smirked and left.

"That apple didn't fall far from the tree," Rhonna said.

"Yes, I see much of Grey Cloak in her. Tell me..." Lythlenion moved farther into the cell and sat on a cot. "Do you like her?"

"I've known worse elves. But yes, I like her. You?"

Lythlenion nodded.

Rhonna sat down beside him. "I guess we wait."

"Yes. After all, this is the moment we've been hoping for."

Zanna knocked on the main entrance to the hold, and Tatum let her out.

"How'd you like your tour?" he asked.

"Relatively grim," she said, "but I don't guess that should be any surprise, given they're dwarves."

Tatum stretched his arms out and yawned. "They're model prisoners." His chair groaned when he sat back down. "They look as happy inside those bars as they do outside. Don't you think?"

"I'd say so." She sat down on the corner of the desk. "Do they ever try to escape? Or have any escaped before?"

Tatum opened the bottom desk drawer, took out a jug, pulled out its cork, and said, "Nah, they can't get out of their own prison." He held up the ring of keys from before. "Without these. At least as far as we know. They're defeated. Besides, the Black Guard and Riskers can handle them. That's why we make an example out of them." He sawed a finger across his throat. "We feed them to the guillotines or the dragons. But tomorrow it's the guillotine for the queen. But don't worry. There won't be any tears. Never seen a dwarf cry or show fear once. At all, ever."

"You sound surprised."

"Well, no, but you'd think one would break down eventually." Tatum took a long drink. "Have some?"

She took the bottle and drank. "Eh, that's bitter."

"Dwarven ale. The best. You should let me take you to their wine cellar, so to speak. It's bigger than the hold. I have to hand it to the dwarves. They're ready for a long siege. It makes me wonder how we overtook them in the first place."

"Perhaps the dragons had something to do with it."

"Aye. Air power. A real difference maker." He put the keys away. "Looking forward to working with you. Do me a favor and tell Edmund I treated you well, will ya?"

"I will." Zanna departed, headed down the streets, and ducked into an alley.

I don't have much time, and I need to get a message to the others.

She opened her satchel, pulled out a vial, and shook the contents.

Hmm. Only one dose left, but this ought to do the trick.

She drank.

34

SAFE HAVEN

GREY CLOAK STOOD ALONE with his hands behind his back, staring into the Eye of the Sky Riders. The image inside the great bowl was an aerial view of the Wizard Watch below Loose Boot. He'd spotted Gossamer disguised as Dirklen having a conversation with Black Frost.

He's going to eat him. I know it.

His fingernails dug into his palms. Too many of his friends had made the ultimate sacrifice. The last thing he wanted was to see it happen again firsthand.

I should have gone, not him.

Zora joined him on the dais. "Oh my. They're talking. Why didn't you say anything?"

"I don't know. My thoughts were elsewhere, I suppose." He took a deep breath through his nose. "This is the moment."

To Grey Cloak's surprise, Black Frost gave Gossamer a nod.

"I think it worked." He smiled. "What do you make of it?"

"He's not dead."

Anya arrived and asked, "What's happening?"

"See for yourself." Grey Cloak pointed at Gossamer. "I believe he did it."

"We'll see." Anya's mouth twitched.

Zora picked at her lip.

Riskers and Black Guard forces started to move south.

"Uh-oh," she said.

"Maybe he convinced him to go the other way," Anya suggested. "After all, Gossamer has betrayed our interest before."

"No, he had to do that," Grey Cloak said as he put his hands on the rim of the bowl. "Look. Black Frost is turning around."

They watched for the longest time.

Black Frost spread his wings and took flight north, toward the mountains of Loose Boot.

"Ha-ha!" Grey Cloak pumped his fist. "He did it! He bought us time!"

Razor and Gorva entered the chamber with curious expressions.

"What's going on?" Razor asked.

"Gossamer did it. He convinced Black Frost to go

north," Grey Cloak replied. "Now all we need to do is get the Apparatus of Ruune built. Zora, we need to use the Medallion of Location. Can you fetch the box?"

"Of course." Zora hurried out of the chamber then returned quickly with Crane's satchel. She dug into it and produced what looked like a jewelry box. "Here it is. What are you going to do with it?"

"We need to see how Dyphestive and Zanna are doing." He set the box down on the rim of the bowl and opened it. Smoke rose from it and quickly dissipated, revealing a bed of black sand. A bright-green dot, like the tip of a firefly's tail, burned on the edge. "Look," he said in a hushed voice.

The green spot started to move.

Grey Cloak did a double take between the locater box and the image in the bowl. "They're moving as one."

The hilltops, farmlands, and lush landscapes of Gapoli whizzed by under their gazes.

The Eye of the Sky Rider passed Portham's rooftops, Havenstock's golden wheat fields, the Iron Hills' boulders, and Sulter Slay's stretches of cracked red clay.

"This is making my eyes hurt," Razor said as he rubbed them and blinked. "I don't think a warrior is meant to view life like this. It doesn't seem real."

"Agreed," Gorva remarked.

Razor's jaw dropped, and he started to speak but opted to close his mouth and smile. Zora smiled at him, but they both averted their eyes from Gorva when she looked between them.

Grey Cloak spotted Dyphestive. "There they are." He spread out the image in the bowl and zoomed closer. "That's my brother, Shannon, and—" He tilted his head. "Chopper?"

"Who's Chopper?" Razor asked. "That fuzzy-faced gnome?"

"Yes, he aided us long ago. I don't see Zanna." He touched the glassy surface of the bowl and panned backward. "Hmmm, it looks like they're hiding in a riverbed. Zooks." He pointed. "Look at that."

A large group of scouts leading dragon hounds—wingless dragons big enough to ride—moved across the dawn, bearing down on Dyphestive's location.

Shaking her head, Anya said, "I think they know they're there. My guess is that they're scouts, and those dragon hounds picked up on their scent. They're like bloodhounds, those nasty things."

"I need to warn them," Grey Cloak said.

"How do you propose to do that?" Zora asked.

He pulled out the Stone of Transport and smirked. "This ought to do the trick." He glanced at the bowl. "Enjoy the show."

Nath appeared beside him, seemingly out of nowhere, tapped Grey Cloak on the shoulder and said, "Before you go, can you return me to the tower. I have a feeling I will be needed there."

Grey Cloak shrugged. "I don't see why not, but let's make it quick." He grabbed Nath's arms. "Hang on you crusty old hermit."

The Stone of Transport pulsed with a dim heartbeat of light, and he vanished with a smile.

Everyone in the chamber gathered around the Eye of the Sky Rider with excitement.

"I don't know why, but this is making me hungry. Does anyone have anything to eat?" Razor asked. "Or drink? Watching this thing is addictive."

"There he is!" Zora said when a dull green light caught her eye.

Grey Cloak reappeared behind the large patrol of soldiers. He picked up a rock and chucked it. It sailed true and smacked a soldier in the back of his helmet.

The soldier stopped in his tracks and turned around, and the soldier behind him marched right into him. A shoving matched started between the two.

Grey Cloak hurled another rock and hit the other soldier in the jaw.

Both soldiers turned around with blood in their eyes and pushed back through the ranks.

Holding his cloak out, Grey Cloak bowed at the patrol

and waved.

The entire Black Guard unit came to a stop. They turned, faced down their enemy, and let their dragon hounds loose.

35

THE DRAGON HOUNDS bore down on Grey Cloak with their jaws wide and slavering. Instead of running, they scuttled with their feet shifting from side to side. The wingless dragons had oversize mouths with multiple sets of sharp teeth that crunched flesh and bone into dust. Like hungry hounds on the hunt, they blazed across the dry landscape, creating a cloud of dust.

My, they're fast.

Grey Cloak backpedaled.

But so am I.

He turned his hips and moved into a full sprint. Looking over his shoulder, he watched the wild pack close in. He stretched stride and angled toward the rocky hills to the east.

Need to get them all as far away as possible.

The leader of the pack gained speed and broke away from the others. It came within one length of Grey Cloak's body.

That one's extra fast!

The dragon hound's black tongue shot out like a whip.

Zooks!

He skipped away, jumped high in the air, and landed at the base of the hills. Hopping from boulder to boulder, he made his way farther up the hill.

Dragon hounds plunged into the hills, claws scraping over the rocks, and spread out like a pride of lions on the hunt.

They're cutting me off.

Grey Cloak ascended, maneuvering toward the peak. He stopped on a jagged set of boulders.

Behind him, the hulking beasts moved slowly, their bullish heads low, and saliva dripped onto the rocks.

The patrol of soldiers ran to catch up, holding their sword belts.

They had Grey Cloak treed like a raccoon.

Here they come.

The dragon hounds came so close that he could smell their hot, rancid breath. They fixed their eyes on him, spread their claws over the rocks, and with their scaly hackles raised, they pounced.

And here I go.

He dropped into a gap between the rocks, used the

Stone of Transport, and vanished. When he reappeared over a hundred yards away, facing the hills, he took a knee.

The patrol searched every crag and nook in the rocks, scratching their heads and shouting curses.

Look at them go. Heh-heh. That should keep them busy.

Grey Cloak had managed to lead them the lesser part of a league away from Dyphestive.

Now it's time to check in with my brother.

He vanished again then appeared in the trench, behind his brother, and tapped him on the shoulder. "Any good news to report?"

Dyphestive looked over his shoulder and said, "No, nothing yet." He started to turn back around but snapped his head back. "Grey! Where'd you come from?"

He pointed toward the sky. "Big Brother's been watching."

"Sweet Gapoli," Shannon said as she moved from her hiding spot. "That's amazing."

"Veritably so!" Chopper said in a chipper voice. He stepped out from under Dyphestive's legs. "Wonderful to see you, Grey Cloak." He blinked and wiggled his eyebrows. "How did you do that?"

Grey Cloak held out the emerald Thunderstone and tossed it up and down. "With a little help from my friend. I have to admit, its use can be addictive."

Chopper's eyes grew as wide as saucers, and his mouth

gaped open. "It's *beautiful*," he said. He wrung his hands and licked his lips. "Might I hold it?"

"I don't think that's a good idea, Chopper. The magic is very strong, and you have to be able to control it."

The sand gnome pinched his thumb and forefinger together, leaving a tiny gap. "Only for a moment. Please."

Grey Cloak put the stone in his inner pockets. "No. So, where do we stand?"

"We're waiting for Zanna to return," Shannon said as she straightened her sword belt. "She's been gone for hours."

"Where's Crane?"

Dyphestive pointed north. "Back in those hills with Tiny."

"Tiny?" Grey Cloak gave an approving nod. "Good."

Chopper crept up on him and started pawing at his cloak.

"Don't do that. Try to pick my pockets, and you might get bitten."

"I love gems, and that one was so beautiful. Sorry." Chopper clamped his hands together, moved into a pocket in the trench, and sat down.

"Anyway," Grey Cloak continued, "I don't know if you noticed, but a large patrol of Black Guards was coming your way."

"We know," Shannon said. "We were about to move on, but I take it you intervened."

He nodded.

"That explains it," she said. "Well done."

Grey Cloak replied, "Well, we can't wait much longer. That patrol will return soon enough, not to mention dragons in the sky. Perhaps I should go after her."

A dust devil appeared above the trench wall and dropped inside.

Dyphestive shielded everyone, pushing them back. "Where in the Flaming Fence did that come from?"

The whirlwind of sand took on a shape. Its gritty fragments became Zanna.

"Whoa!" Dyphestive said. He poked her shoulder. "Is that you?"

"Of course it's me. I used a Vial of Wind to whisk me out," she said as she straightened her hair.

"Why didn't you use it to get in?" Shannon asked.

"It was a last resort, and I had no other way." Zanna leaned over and spotted her son. "Grey! When did you arrive?"

"Moments ago. Did you find Rhonna?"

Zanna nodded. "Her and Lythlenion and plenty of willing dwarves who can build the apparatus."

Dyphestive clasped his hands together. "Yes. How do we get them out?"

"They're kept in the hold," Zanna said. "And I haven't figured that out yet."

"No need," Grey Cloak said with a smile. He held out

the Stone of Transport. "With this, we can pop in and pop them right out."

Zanna smirked. "Brilliant, son. But you don't know where to go."

"No, but you do. After the first use, you'll quickly grasp it. Envision where you want to go, and you'll be there in a blink."

"If you say so." Zanna held out her hands. "No sense in waiting any longer."

Grey Cloak tossed her the stone.

Chopper jumped into its path with a wild smile and snatched it. "It's mine!" he said and disappeared.

Everyone's jaws dropped.

Grey Cloak looked about and spun around. "No! Chopper, come back!"

After several minutes of calling to him and looking high and low, Dyphestive said, "What do we do?"

"Don't panic. We will find that stone." Grey Cloak's jaw muscles clenched. "Zooks. He could be anywhere, but he'll show up eventually. Rhonna's rescue will have to wait until then."

With a serious expression, Zanna said, "We don't have until then."

"Why is that?"

"Because Rhonna is slated to be executed in the morning."

36

BACK IN THE hills near Crane's wagon, Tiny said, "I can find Chopper. I know he loves the stones. He hunts them all the time and has many stored in many places." The cyclops scratched the little horns of armor on the back of his skull. "But it will take a while."

"How long is a while?" Grey Cloak asked.

Tiny shrugged. "There are a bunch of nooks in these hills where he likes to hide. I'll search them all and find him. Perhaps I'll find him in the first hole."

The sun had risen above the hills.

"Zanna, when are they going to execute Rhonna?"

"From what I overheard, it will be midday."

Grey Cloak grimaced. "Anvils. That doesn't give us a lot of time."

"No, and we need to get out the other dwarven engineers to build the apparatus." Zanna shook her head. "I have a few more vials at my disposal, and your pockets should be filled as well. A shame you didn't think to bring the Scarf of Shadows. That would have been helpful."

"I didn't think I'd need it." He gave her an aggravated look. "Who could have foreseen that a grubby little gnome would snatch the stone away?"

"Well, he was acting squirrely when he saw the stone," Dyphestive said.

"Thanks, brother."

"You're welcome."

"I'm going to look for Chopper." Tiny thumped his chest and moseyed down the trail with his long arms swinging. "I'll find him."

"We don't have time to wait," Zanna said.

"Agreed." Grey Cloak checked his inner pockets. Tatiana had loaded him up with vials long ago and given him a small scroll of instructions. Zanna had done something similar when he and Dyphestive were turned into stone. He removed a handful of vials and asked, "Where is that scroll?"

"I can read them." Zanna scooped up some vials. "Batram and I went through some very heavy negotiations." She eyeballed one after the other. "Fire breath. Immunity. Revival. Haste. I don't see how some of these will help. Shrinking." Her eyes widened. "These are the potions I bartered for. That giant eight-armed rodent did a switch!"

Grey Cloak grinned. "Well, look who's been swindled. Well-played, Mother."

"I can't believe he fooled me."

"Well, you can't do much about it now." He took out a few more potions. "I think this is giantus. Remember that one, brother?"

"Aye, I do. The ettin," Dyphestive said.

"Well, most of these potions are worthless for our cause." Grey Cloak stuffed his hand into more pockets. "But I do have the Figurine of Heroes. Perhaps it will make for a distraction."

Zanna shrugged.

"Speaking of distractions," Shannon said from her lookout position on the rocks, "the Black Patrol is coming this way."

"Fantastic," Grey Cloak said sarcastically.

"I hate to say this, but we might not be able to save Rhonna. If that is the case, we can rescue the other dwarves," Zanna stated. "I'm sure she would understand."

Grey Cloak and Dyphestive glowered down at her and said, "That's not an option."

She raised her hands in defeat. "Fine. No need to bear down on me. I'm sure we'll think of something."

Crane sat on the bench seat of his wagon, staring at the clouds with a puzzled expression. Dyphestive paced from one side of the trail to the other, rubbing his chin. Zanna squatted and drew in the dirt with a stick.

Grey Cloak locked his fingers behind his head and sighed. *Think, Grey Cloak. Think. There must be a way to do this. There always is.*

"Excuse me, but the troops have picked up the pace," Shannon said. "My guess is those dragon hounds picked up our scent."

"Anvils," Dyphestive muttered.

"I have an idea," Crane said brightly.

Everyone turned his direction.

He raised his hands and spread out his chubby fingers. "We get captured. Steal some horses, rescue Rhonna and the dwarves, and ride out like a clap of thunder."

"We can't outrun the dragons," Grey Cloak said.

"No, but we can fight them," Dyphestive added. "And maybe Tiny will find Chopper in the meantime."

"That's some thin ice you're talking about," Grey Cloak said, but his wheels began spinning. "But if we get inside and I have my cloak, well..." He frowned. "Zooks, if I only had a better way to hide."

"You do!" Crane said. He waved them all to the wagon.

They surrounded it.

Crane leaned over his bench seat, dug his thick fingers between the gap in the planks, and tried to pull them up. He panted and grunted, and his face turned beet red.

"I think I understand." Grey Cloak reached into the wagon and lifted one of the planks. "Well, will you look at that. A false bottom there all the time. It covers the entire bed."

Crane eagerly nodded and caught his breath. "We can stow your weapons in there."

Grey Cloak reached deep into the bay. "Not only that, but you can fit me in there as well."

"I think we'll both fit," Zanna said.

"So, what do you say? Want to go for it?" Crane asked.

Grey Cloak climbed into the wagon. "Why not? I'll take my chances."

37

THE BLACK GUARD patrol took Dyphestive, Crane, and Shannon prisoner. They seized the wagon and had a dragon hound tow it. With their hands bound in front of them, the prisoners were marched toward the main northern gate of Dwarf Skull.

After they'd been walking awhile, Crane fell to his knees then hit the dirt face-first. He groaned like he was a hundred years old.

An orcen Black Guard soldier pulled Crane up by his hair. "Stay on your feet, or you'll be dead meat."

"I'm sorry. But I'm an old man with a fat body. Look at these scrawny legs. They can barely carry me. That's why I ride in a wagon. Can't I ride in the wagon, sir? Please?"

The orc clamped his hand around Crane's neck. "I

should break you in half and feed you to the dragon hounds."

"Leave him alone, will you?" Dyphestive interjected.

"Huh?" The orc swung his gaze toward Dyphestive. "What comment was that, Blondie?"

"Look at him," Dyphestive said. "He can barely walk, and it's only slowing us all down. Don't you want to get out of the sun?"

"Shaddup." The orc wiped his nose and shoved Crane toward the wagon, eyeing two of his men. "Toss him in the back, but keep an eye on him."

"I don't think he's going to escape," Dyphestive commented.

The orc took off his helmet, revealing his lumpy bald head, and whacked Dyphestive in the face. "I said shaddup!"

Dyphestive wobbled down to one knee, though it was an act. He forced himself back up and spit blood. "I don't know what we did, but we were on our way to Dwarf Skull. No need to take us prisoner, as I tried to explain."

"We'll let the commander decide your fate," the orcen leader said. He eyeballed Shannon. "Look at her in Honor Guard armor. There will be no fooling me."

"Plenty of soldiers left their positions to join the Black Guard. I'm one of them," Dyphestive said.

"Keep this patrol moving!"

The soldiers resumed their trek.

The orc jammed his helmet on, and the leather straps dangled by his chin. "We don't take anyone. You have to be vetted like the rest of us. And I don't care for the looks of either of you. Something stinks."

"We haven't done anything. If it's the man in the cloak you're looking for—"

Grabbing Dyphestive by his vest, the orc asked, "Did you see a man in a cloak?"

"Actually, an elf." He rolled his eyes. "I tried to tell you. An elf in a dark cloak showed up and stole our gear and our horse. That's why we were stranded. Did it while we slept." He nodded toward Crane. "It was the old man's turn to watch. Woke up with my gear gone and the fat old fellow snoring like a bear."

"Where did the elf go?"

"North, I assume. I don't know. Why? Did he steal from you?" Dyphestive asked. He had the orc's full attention.

"Nah! But he created a dustup. Very peculiar. Moved like a mirage. Sent us on a wild chase." The orc caught himself opening up to the prisoner. "Why am I telling you this?" He stormed toward the front, shouting, "Everyone, check your gear! Make sure nothing is missing!"

Dyphestive looked over at Shannon. She smiled, and he winked at her.

"Well, we haven't been this close in a while," Zanna said to Grey Cloak. Both of them lay flat on their backs with their noses practically touching the false floor of the wagon. It was dark, but faint beams of light bled through the cracks. "Not since you were—"

"Don't say it."

"What did you think I was going to say?"

"In the womb."

She chuckled. "No, I wasn't going to say that. I was going to say since you were an infant. We weren't always separated, you know."

"We weren't?"

"No, of course not. But you would have been too young to remember."

The wagon rattled over the bumpy road, pitching from side to side on occasion. He slid toward his mother and her, to him.

"Well, this is awkward."

"And hot," she said.

"Really? A shame. The Cloak of Legends gives me a great deal of comfort."

"Like being in the womb?"

"Funny, but I wouldn't know. No one can remember that far back, and I'm glad I don't."

"Psst!" Crane's eye showed through a small knothole. "We're entering the city. Catch up on old times later and clam up."

The light from the cracks dimmed for a moment as the wagon rolled underneath the main gate.

Grey Cloak had been to Dwarf Skull before, briefly, and Zanna had already made herself familiar. All they needed to do was find Rhonna before it was too late.

The last part of the journey was the most agonizing, as they rolled over the stone through the city.

"Are we ever going to stop?" he asked quietly.

As if he'd commanded it, the wagon stopped. He thought he could see his mother smile in the dimness.

He touched her hand and squeezed. "Let's do this."

38

AFTER MARCHING THROUGH DWARF SKULL, Dyphestive and Shannon were forced into a confinement facility, practically shoved through the front door.

A rugged man was standing over a desk. His eyes widened, and he hid a jug of wine behind his back.

"Tatum!" the lead orc said. "Are you drinking on duty again?"

"What if I am, Bazak?"

Bazak grinned. "Then you'd better have saved some for me. Toss me that jug. It's been a rough morning." He tipped his head at the other soldiers. "Put them in a lockup."

"Hold on," Tatum said and tossed the jug.

Bazak snatched it. "Don't give me grief. These two claim to be recruits for the Black Guard. Found them in the north hills, acting squirrely. Not sure what to believe." He drank.

Wine sloshed over his scruffy beard and down his chin. He finished the bottle and tossed it back. "I owe you one."

"I'll say. You didn't have to drink it all. I don't have any more in my stash. And I was going off duty." Tatum frowned and set the jug down on the end of his desk. He crossed his arms and eyed Dyphestive. "He's a big one."

"Mouthy too. Listen, lock them down until we track down Sergeant Fitzgerald, and he can deal with them. I have to go."

"Go? Why?"

"I lost one of them. The fat, old one. Can you believe that?" Bazak scoffed. "Said he couldn't walk and slipped out of my grasp. I told my men to keep an eye on him." He glowered at Dyphestive. "You said not to worry about it, and look what happened. You're up to something, but we'll get to the bottom of it." He flicked his index finger out. "I'd better not miss the execution." He turned his attention back to Tatum. "Have they been taken to the block yet?"

"No. I was expecting the executioners' guards to arrive when you popped in. It won't be long, though. I'd get stepping if you don't want to miss it." He grabbed a key ring from a peg on the wall and eyed the other soldiers. "Put them in the back lockup and bring me the keys. I'll stand here and wait for my relief and the executioners to arrive."

"Don't take your eyes off of them," Bazak warned him.

"I won't. Go. And you owe me a bottle. No, you owe me two!"

Dyphestive and Shannon were forced into the holding cell with their hands still bound together.

"Say, can we have these links removed?"

"No!" Tatum shouted. "You're someone else's problem. Not mine. Let Fitzgerald deal with it." The floorboards creaked as he paced. "Can't believe they're holding me up like this. I want to get to the executioners' block early and be in the front. Bloody biscuits. Of all the days to be late."

The planks of the wagon's false floor slid back, revealing Crane's chronically genial expression. "Ho! Ho!" he said. "As they say, the coast is clear."

Grey Cloak was first to squeeze out of the gap. "Took you long enough."

"But was there any doubt?"

"Yes," Zanna said as she rose with the help of both men's hands. "Where are we?"

"The stables, I presume." Crane started putting the boards back into place. "Can't you smell the sweet aroma of manure?"

"Where are the soldiers?" Grey Cloak asked.

Crane waved his hands. "Don't worry about them. I've sent them on a wild goose chase." He did a little dance. "My feet are much fleeter than they realized." He rubbed his hands together. "Dyphestive and Shannon were taken to the hold. So, what's the plan?"

Zanna handed him a vial. "This is for fleetness. Hitch up a horse and be ready. It will be us and many passengers."

"I had a chance to scout the area. We aren't far from the block," Crane said.

"The block?" Grey Cloak asked as he moved toward the exit.

"That's where they do the executions. Plenty are gathered in the streets. Mostly soldiers. Very much like a festival but grim." Crane took out a pipe and stuffed tobacco into it. "A bit sad."

"That's because they're going to kill Rhonna. You remember her, don't you?" Grey Cloak asked.

"Ah, the dwarven woman. A real beauty. Is she married?"

"She won't be anything if we don't save her." Grey Cloak pointed at Crane. "Get the wagon ready. Come on, Mom."

Zanna smiled.

"What's that look for?"

"You called me Mom. It tickled my heart."

"Well, Mom..." He offered his elbow. "Will you do me the pleasure of helping me save my other mother, Rhonna?"

She took his arm. "I'd be honored."

"But don't you dare tell Rhonna I called you Mother."

"Oh, I won't." Zanna led the way into the streets.

Crane had been right. It was primarily soldiers, numbering in the hundreds, moving in the same direction. Some were common folk, too, most likely family members of the officers and other workers who were hired to keep the city operational, since the dwarves had abandoned them. Dwarf Skull was under full operation but by a skeleton crew.

With Zanna still in a Black Guard uniform, no one paid Grey Cloak or her any mind. They kept to the sidewalks and made their way to the hold.

"I take it you know where the hold is?" Grey Cloak asked.

"We're close. This is the southern quadrant, and we'll have to make our escape through the north. Or the closest gate. Getting beyond the dragons, well, that will take some doing."

"Agreed, but one thing at a time. Let's get Rhonna first."

Zanna pointed at a building with a well-marked sign chiseled out of stone and painted black and red. "That's the hold. Shouldn't be hard to find Dyphestive if he's in there. They're a bit lazy."

They started across the street, but a half-naked man stumbled into their path. He looked Zanna dead in the eye and screamed.

39

———

GREY CLOAK CLAMPED his hand over the smallish man's mouth and dragged him away from the main road. "Who is this?" he asked Zanna.

"A new acquaintance of mine. How are you feeling, PeeWee?"

"Don't talk to him. He'll scream."

Zanna drew her dagger and placed the tip underneath PeeWee's eye. "No, he won't. Let him speak."

Grey Cloak removed his hand but kept PeeWee's arms locked behind his back. "He reeks of ale."

"Yes, he had quite a party last night," Zanna said. "Didn't you?"

"I don't remember most of it, thanks to you," PeeWee said. "I'm in a lot of trouble, and you have my uniform. Please give it back, and I won't say a word. I swear it."

"Sorry, but we have more pressing matters at hand." Zanna looked about. "And I can't risk letting you open your mouth."

"L-Listen to me. I know y-you aren't one of the Black Guard, and I don't want to be either. But what choice do I have?" He licked his lips. "Why don't you take me with you? I want out of this place."

"Not an option," Grey Cloak said.

"Certainly I can help in some manner. Please, I might as well be dead. Sergeant Edmund will probably put me on the block next for what you've put me through. I'd rather die trying to live than live wanting to die. I hate this place."

Zanna gave the young man a sympathetic look.

"We have enough on our plates," Grey Cloak said. "Whatever you're thinking, stop."

"I don't know. He might be of some use to us. And we can't leave him dead in the street. It would draw too much attention."

Grey Cloak spotted a pair of soldiers walking toward them. "Company is coming. We need to move on."

"They aren't here for us. They're going to the execution. Lie down, both of you."

The Black Guards walked by and looked them over.

Zanna nodded at them and said in a manly voice, "Someone had a little too much fun last night."

"Need a hand?" one of the soldiers asked.

"No, I already have some help coming. Go on. Don't

miss the execution. Hopefully, I'll have this mess taken care of before it happens."

They nodded and moved back into the main street.

"Lords of thunder, I only want to crawl under my cot and die," PeeWee said. "I feel sick."

Grey Cloak popped up. "Don't barf on my boots."

A chorus of cheers rose from the soldiers in the streets.

"Let me check it out."

Zanna nodded. "I'll deal with PeeWee."

Grey Cloak moved to the end of the street, stepped onto the sidewalk, and rose on tiptoe. He could see the block, a raised platform like the ones they'd used to make the gallows in Monarch City. Instead of a set of ropes, there were guillotines.

Everyone's attention was drawn to the trio of men standing atop the platform. They wore bronze helmets shaped like skulls with white horns. Their dingy, blood-stained cloaks hung over their heavy shoulders, showing bare, muscular, tattooed arms. Frayed rope belts were tied around their waists. Grim and silent, they faced the throng of blood-hungry men and nodded. They made their way toward the steps that led down through the block.

Grey Cloak hurried back to Zanna. "I think it's about to happen."

PeeWee peered over his shoulder. "Did the executioners arrive? Ah, I'm going to miss it."

"Have you done something with him?"

Zanna sighed. She put her dagger away and pinched PeeWee's cheek. "Sorry to put you through all this, but it appears I don't have a choice. I'll leave your uniform in the hold."

"The hold?" PeeWee blinked. "Why there?"

Zanna's fingers brightened like candlelight, then she touched PeeWee on the shoulder and zapped him.

His eyes widened, and he slumped over.

"Are you worried he'll be found and rat us out?" Grey Cloak asked.

"We are too far along to worry about that now." She gazed at PeeWee with sympathy and stood. "Let's go."

Grey Cloak gave her a funny look.

"What? I feel sorry for him."

Grey Cloak smirked. "You?"

She gave him a playful shove in the back. "Lead the way, son."

The executioners walked down a path toward the hold, where the masses had parted. With their helmets, they stood head and shoulders above most men.

Looking back over his shoulder as they moved down the sidewalk, Grey Cloak asked, "What do you think? Should we wait or go in?"

"We'll have more control if we can slip inside."

"It's going to be hard with all eyes on the door. We'll

need a distraction. Not a big one but one long enough for everyone to look away." Grey Cloak spotted an abandoned cart half-loaded with straw. "Wait here. I think I can handle it."

40

INSIDE THE HOLDING CELL, Shannon nudged Dyphestive with her elbow. "Look there."

He had already turned his head toward the sound of the commotion. From the cell, they had a partial view down the hall toward the front entrance. Tatum was talking to some people. He and Shannon craned their necks to hear.

"It's about time," Tatum said in his coarse voice. "I was beginning to wonder whether we were going to have the execution today or tomorrow."

In a deep, muffled voice, one of the executioners responded, "Release the prisoners."

"Well, now that you're here, I'd be obliged to," Tatum said sarcastically.

The speaking executioner grabbed Tatum by the collar

of his breastplate, lifted him off his toes, and pushed him against the door.

"Strong," Shannon uttered.

"E-Easy, now," Tatum stammered. "No disrespect. I'm an avid supporter of your work. I swear it."

The executioner dropped him. "Do it," he commanded.

"I think that's our sign," Dyphestive said. "Excuse me."

Shannon stepped back from the door and asked, "What are you doing?"

Dyphestive grabbed the metal bars. "I'm going to nab Rhonna before they take her out of here."

Shannon leaned back against the wall with her arms crossed over her chest. "You're going to open that door? That dwarven steel is over an inch thick."

"I know." His knuckles turned white as he tried to pull the bars apart. "Hurk!" Dyphestive's biceps swelled like two ripe melons ready to burst.

She pushed off the wall. "I think they're moving."

He groaned and gasped. The metal began to bend.

"Anvils, your neck is turning red. Is your head going to explode?"

"No. I've handled thicker metal."

The long shafts of metal started to spread apart, groaning. One of the bars popped out of the hole in the top. Dyphestive bent it down until it kissed the floor.

"Whoa," Shannon said. "You should do carnivals."

He grabbed the other bar and bent it down to the floor

as well, creating a gap big enough for him to squeeze through.

"What about the executioners?" she asked.

"Stay behind me. Once the dwarves are out, we'll strike hard and fast."

"I like it."

Dyphestive stepped through the gap and moved forward on cat's feet.

The door that led into the hold swung open.

Dyphestive held his fingers to his lips and mouthed, "Wait."

"Ah, there they are! Count them all!" Tatum said. "Queen Rhonna and the six dwarves. Well, er, plus an orc. They're all yours, fellas. I mean executioners. Hold on, Let me test their bonds. These dwarves can get squirrely when their time is up. As you know, of course. But they all want to die fighting."

"We'll handle it," the executioner said in his haunting voice. "This is our custom, not yours, jailer."

"Of course."

Dyphestive spotted Rhonna and the dwarves spilling into the room. He eyed the door and nodded at Shannon.

She snuck over to the door, placed both hands on it, and slammed it shut on Tatum's arm.

The jailer screamed.

Dyphestive moved in on the nearest executioner and walloped him in his soft belly.

The executioner groaned as he crumpled to the floor, holding his gut. "Aargh, that felt like a mule kicking me."

"Get out of here!" one of the other executioners said. "We need to sound the alarm. Esca—oof!"

Rhonna had rammed her head into the man's groin.

Dyphestive ripped the final one's helmet off and punched him in his ugly face.

All three executioners were down, but Tatum was still screaming, until Shannon stole his dagger from his belt and shoved it against his throat. "Be silent, or I'll silence you."

The door opened, and Dyphestive hid behind it. Two people stepped in the room, and he quickly shut the door behind them. "Grey! Zanna! What a fine place for a reunion!" He took two giant strides over to Rhonna and picked her up. "It's good to see you!"

"Easy, biggun. It's good to see you, too, but you don't have to pop me. Now, get these shackles off."

One of the executioners started to get up.

Lythlenion kicked him in the gut. "I've always wanted to do that."

"Let's throw them in the hold," Dyphestive said.

Shannon opened a cell door and shoved Tatum inside with a quick kick in the seat of his pants. "Enjoy your stay."

Dyphestive and Lythlenion dragged the executioners across the floor. "It's good to see you, old friend," Lythlenion commented.

"You too."

"Hold a moment," Rhonna said. "What do you have? Anvils for brains?"

"Of course not," Grey Cloak said. He squeezed her shoulder. "We're going to need their clothing. They'll be perfect disguises. Who knows. We might slip right out of here after all."

Dyphestive, Lythlenion, and Shannon dressed in the executioners' gear.

Zanna grabbed all sets of the key rings to the hold and wiggled them in front of Rhonna. "Why don't we lock them up in the hold, and so long as we have the opportunity, maybe you want to let a few more of your brethren go."

Rhonna winked. "I like the way you think. Braath and Muaug, take those keys. You know what to do."

Grey Cloak peeked through the wooden blinds. "It looks like they've doused the fire I started. It's smoky, but they're getting restless. Huh. A few Riskers are investigating. We'd better get this underway."

"So, what's the plan?" Dyphestive asked.

"They want a show." Grey Cloak smirked. "We'll give them a show they'll never forget."

41

DYPHESTIVE LED the disguised executioners and their five prisoners out of the hold and was greeted by a rousing chorus of cheers and threats.

"Kill the dwarves!"

"Shave their beards!"

"Make them tell you where their gold is first!"

Rhonna and her quartet of brethren shuffled along with their hands bound behind their backs. Zanna, still disguised as a Black Guard, brought up the rear.

As the train of prisoners waded into the crowd of parting soldiers, Grey Cloak slipped down the sidewalk and made his way toward the stables. The smell of burnt wood from the cart he'd set on fire still lingered in the air. Smoke drifted through the throng.

I made quite a stink, didn't I?

Dyphestive moseyed through the streets with his massive arms raised in the air. The soldiers hurled rotten vegetables and other scraps at the dwarves. When Dyphestive dropped his arms, Lythlenion raised his in a slow and eerie motion.

The Black Guard ate it up.

So far, so good. Keep up the ruse while we still have surprise on our side.

Grey Cloak picked up the pace as more soldiers hurried down the main street toward the block.

He slipped into the barn and found Crane sitting on the drop door in the wagon. "Is it time? Do you have it ready to go?"

Crane shrugged. "You could say that."

"What do you mean?"

"There weren't many options to choose from in these stables." Crane slipped down to the ground. "But he'll have to do."

Grey Cloak moved to the front of the wagon. A dapple-gray horse with his better days behind him was hitched up. He had a dip in his back, and his ribs were showing. "Zooks! What is this? Can it even pull the wagon?"

"Of course he can." Crane scratched the old horse behind the ears. "And he's not an it. He has a name. Charger."

"Really? And how did you come to know that name?"

Crane made kissing sounds to the horse and fed him an apple. "He told me."

With his hands on his hips, and shaking his head, Grey Cloak said, "This is not going to work. If Chopper hadn't stolen the stone, this would be as easy as pie! We're better off running out of here. Horseshoes!"

"Dwarves aren't very fast. Have you seen them run? They look like giant groundhogs running on their hind legs. Have some faith in old Charger. He's got some fight left in him. I can see it."

Grey Cloak clenched his jaw. "Fine. Get this wagon out on the road. I'll flag down Dyphestive."

"Not a problem. Come on, Charger. It's time to go on a little run." He led the horse and wagon backward out of the barn. "Good boy."

"This might be a disaster in the making. Who am I kidding? It *is* a disaster." Grey Cloak rushed outside and made his way back toward the crowd.

With the skull helm on, Dyphestive looked like a giant among men, and Lythlenion was little smaller. Shannon, a strapping woman, appeared to be pulling off her part as an executioner thanks to Dyphestive and Lythlenion drawing all the attention to themselves.

Grey Cloak moved up the sidewalk and tried to catch Dyphestive's eye. His brother swung his head in his direction and nodded.

"Whew!" Grey Cloak spotted a trio of Riskers marching down the street from the opposite side. "Oh no."

The Riskers were in full suits of blackened dragon-scale armor and wore open-faced helmets with wings on the side. All three were large men with scowls on their faces. They made themselves comfortable on the sidewalk and carefully observed the ceremony.

And now it gets tricky.

The Riskers murmured among themselves. One of them flagged an officer from the Black Guard down and appeared to be chewing the man out as he pointed at the block and the executioners.

Grey Cloak narrowed his eyes and tried to read the man's lips.

Get this over with. Is that what he said? Zooks. He's not one for ceremonies.

One of the other Riskers laid a hand on the talking Risker's shoulder.

And he says, "Let them celebrate. It will be over soon enough. Might as well enjoy ourselves." And the nosy one responds with a shrug and sends the officer along. Whew! I think that almost made me sweat. As if I didn't have enough problems to solve.

Crane backed the wagon into the street, facing the north gate looming in the distance. He nodded at Grey Cloak, jostled the reins, and said something unintelligible. Charger started slowly walking backward.

It's showtime.

Dyphestive turned and started leading the prisoners down the street toward the wagon, swaying his raised arms from side to side.

The soldiers chanted, "Death to the queen! Death to the queen!"

Dyphestive approached the wagon and opened the back gate, still waving his arms back and forth. He made a cutting motion across his throat.

The bloodthirsty crowd yelled at the top of their lungs. "Death to the queen! Death to Rhonna!" they chanted.

Lythlenion and Shannon lifted the dwarves into the wagon.

Dyphestive snatched up Rhonna and held her up by the armpits like a child.

The soldiers screamed and cajoled, gathering around the wagon.

Grey Cloak slipped into the seat with Crane. "Get this thing rolling," he said through the side of his mouth.

Lythlenion and Shannon climbed into the wagon and stood with their arms crossed.

Charger tugged the wagon forward at an agonizingly slow pace, and Zanna took a seat on the open back gate.

The soldiers walked behind the wagon, chanting and cheering for death, as they all paraded down the street.

"This is awkward," Grey Cloak said. "Can't we go any faster?"

"No need to tip our cap yet," Crane said. "Look ahead. The gate is still open."

"Then what? Are we going to crawl away from the dragon we have to contend with?"

"Don't worry. You'll figure something out," Crane replied with a cheerful smile.

Rhonna turned around and griped at Dyphestive, "What sort of rescue is this? Did halfling children come up with it?"

"You'll have to ask Grey," Dyphestive said, still holding her up. "You're getting heavy. Have you gained weight?"

The orcen patrol leader Bazak pushed his way to the front of the parade. A scowl grew on his face. "I know that wagon." He moved over to the side and glowered at Crane. "You!"

Crane waved his fingers at Bazak.

"You're the old man we've been looking for. Get out of that wagon!" He spotted Grey Cloak. "And I know that cloak. You're the one in the plains who kept disappearing. I knew you were up to something." He raised his blade. "Sound the alarm! These people are imposters! Get them!"

42

"Why did you wave at him?" Grey Cloak asked Crane.

"I don't know. I was only being courteous." Crane snapped the reins.

"Never mind that now. Get this mule moving!"

Charger sped up to a trot, but the soldiers closed right in on the wagon.

Someone blew a warning horn. The sound carried down the road, bouncing off the buildings. Another horn sounded farther down the street. Far ahead, the portcullis of the northern gate closed.

"Zooks! We're trapped!" Grey Cloak said.

"Maybe so, but Charger is speeding up," Crane said with a flick of the reins. "Go, boy! Go!" His head shifted from side to side, looking around. "Someone find my horse whip. That might make him go faster."

"Where is it?" Shannon asked as she took off her helmet and hurled it at the pursuers, knocking a few of them over.

"I don't know. Ah, check between the floorboards."

The soldiers sprinted in front of the wagon.

"This is embarrassing," Grey Cloak said. "If we can't outrun the Black Guard, how are we going to outrun dragons?" He grabbed the Rod of Weapons. "Mother, it's time to do some damage!"

"Time indeed." Zanna's fingernails brightened, and streams of energy from her fingers smote the nearest soldiers and made the rest scatter.

Grey Cloak laid into the soldiers running alongside the wagon with a flurry of blue fire. From the nearest to the farthest back, he hit them one by one, sending five men stumbling.

The soldiers backed away, but Bazak's voice could be heard from a mile away. "Cowards! Get after them! They don't have anywhere to go!"

The wagon rumbled along, but Zanna pointed at the trio from earlier. "The Riskers are onto us. Look!"

Three middling dragons scurried over the rooftops and jumped down into the street. The Riskers climbed into their saddles and prepared their bows. Their arrows' tips glowed with fire and were aimed at the wagon.

The first Risker fired, and the arrow streaked across the road.

Zanna snatched it out of the air, inches from Lythlenion's face.

"I would have ducked, but I didn't want it to strike anyone else," he said.

"It's fine."

They were closing in on the northern gate, but the portcullis closed.

"You need to turn, Crane!" Grey Cloak said.

"It won't make any difference. I need my horse whip!"

Shannon and the dwarves ripped up the false floor.

One of the dwarves removed a plank and chucked it down the road, hitting a pair of soldiers in the legs. "Find that lash!"

The dragons roared, rustled their wings, and gave chase.

Suddenly, the dwarven prisoners poured out of the hold. The war-ready, wild-eyed dwarven soldiers scurried across the streets like a swarm of bearded ants. They started at the bottom, seizing the dragons' legs, climbing one over another, and attacking both dragons and riders in bunches.

"Look at that!" Rhonna bellowed. "The revolt begins! This is the day I've been waiting for! Take it to them, kindred!"

The dwarves riding in the wagon hung out over the sides, cheering and hooting.

Bazak slowed his pursuit and turned. "No!" Soldiers

rushed by him, but he grabbed them and said, "Turn around! Turn around! Forget about the wagon! The prisoners are loose!"

Shannon finally found the horse lash and handed it to Crane. "Is this what you're looking for?"

Flames lit in his eyes. "You bet, darling!" He grabbed the whip and cracked it, making it catch fire. "Here comes the Flaming Thunder!"

He cracked the whip on Charger's back, and the beast lurched forward. Flames spread from the lash to the horse's hooves. Even the wagon wheels caught fire.

Charger let out a frightening whinny and transformed into a muscular thoroughbred of tremendous size. They gained speed and thundered toward the northern gate.

The soldiers, barring their path with their spears lowered, turned as white as sheets and jumped aside.

"Crane!" Grey Cloak said as they raced toward the portcullis. "That gate's made of iron!"

"No problem!" Crane cracked the lash again. "Show them what an old man can do, Charger!"

"Brace yourself!" Grey Cloak said.

Everyone ducked.

Charger burst through the portcullis like it was nothing more than a waterfall.

Grey Cloak uncovered his eyes and looked about. Dwarf Skull was shrinking in the distance. "Ha-ha!"

Everyone belted out triumphant cries.

Dyphestive and Lythlenion chucked their skull helmets away.

Grey Cloak stood. "Crane! That was unbelievable!"

"That's what she said," he replied with a smile. "Where to?"

"East," Grey Cloak said as he looked back once more.

Grand and middling dragons came together on Dwarf Skull's northern wall. At least a score could be seen. Riskers climbed into their saddles. One of the men blew a battle horn, then the dragons spread their wings and flew into pursuit.

Everyone stared at Grey Cloak.

He nudged Crane. "How fast can Charger go?"

Crane looked over his shoulder. "Fast but not that fast. And he can't run forever, you know."

43

Grey Cloak counted the enemy dragons chasing them . "Nineteen, twenty, twenty-one. That's a lot!"

"We can take them," Dyphestive said. He was hunkered down in the middle of the wagon like a giant bullfrog. The rushing wind stirred his stiff locks of blond hair. He clung to the wagon's rim while dwarves clung to him. "But only if we have to stop. How fast are we going?"

Crane shrugged. He turned and gazed at his pursuers. "We'll give them a run for it, but I'm not promising anything."

Charger sped across the dry landscape at twice the speed of any fast horse, snorting flame and smoke. The muscles underneath his shiny coat labored. His burning hooves pounded over the rocky road.

The chase went on for the better part of a league.

"They're gaining on us!" Rhonna said as she rummaged through the false bottom, looking for a weapon. "They'll cook us alive if they cut us off."

"We aren't cut off yet, Rhonna!" Zanna shouted as the wind blew her hair across her face. She brushed it out of her eyes. "Don't worry. Grey Cloak will think of something."

"Of course I will."

Or will I? Twenty-one dragons. Twenty-one Riskers. That's more than three against one. We're going to have to even the odds somehow.

He reached into the pockets of his cloak and removed the Figurine of Heroes. The featureless humanoid shape was as smooth as polished glass.

I didn't fare too well with this last time, but I don't think I have a choice.

He dropped it back into his pocket and tapped Crane on the shoulder. "How's Charger doing?"

"He might have another league in him. My powers don't last forever, and we're giving it all we have."

Squinting, Grey Cloak noticed more hills in the distance. "Go there. We can fight better if we spread out and find cover in the rocks."

"Aye, aye! Away, Charger. Away!" Crane bellowed.

Zanna climbed over the dwarves and joined Grey Cloak. "They'll be upon us soon enough. They're waiting for us to slow. And in case you hadn't noticed, seven of those dragons are grands."

"It's hard not to notice, but we're heading toward the hills, trying to even the odds." He jabbed his finger forward. "If we make it, we'll battle in those rocks. Now might be a good time to distribute those potions. We'll need every advantage to get an edge."

"I don't think those dwarves will go for it."

"Tell Rhonna." He winked. "She'll handle it."

They traveled another mile, then Charger started to slow. Sweat covered his back.

"We aren't going to make it to the hills, are we?" Grey Cloak asked.

"Come on, Charger! Come on!" Crane yelled with a crack of his lash. "You can do it, boy!"

The big steed snorted fire and gained speed.

"He's doing it! He's doing it!" Dyphestive said. He reached between the planks and grabbed the Iron Sword. "When this wagon stops, I'll be ready!"

"We'll all be ready," Rhonna said as she took potion vials from Zanna. "Not my form of ale, but we'll do what we have to."

"Almost there!" Crane said. "Almost there! Go, Charger! Go!"

The flames around the wheels and the horse's hooves began to fade.

"Oh no. We aren't going to make it," Grey Cloak said.

The quicker middling dragons spread out and closed in on the wagon. One of them darted straight overhead.

"Not good!"

Then the dragon in the front dive-bombed the wagon.

"Crane, watch out!"

He jerked the reins, and Charger pulled left, but he was too slow. The middling dragon collided with the steed.

"Hold on!" Grey Cloak said.

The wagon rose, toppled to one side, and skidded across the hot ground.

Grey Cloak jerked Crane out of his seat as he jumped and landed on his feet. He watched the dwarves roll across the ground like tumbleweeds. They popped up on their knees with dirt in their beards.

"Everyone, take cover by the wagon," Dyphestive said. "Stay together."

The wheels on the top side were still spinning as the mystical flames died out.

Seven dragons landed while others circled above.

The Riskers and dragons on the ground surrounded them in a ring of wings and scales. The great lizards huffed out plumes of fire. The Riskers sat tall in their saddles with triumphant grins.

One of the Riskers rode on a grand dragon with grass-green scales. He had a full beard with braids in it, like many dwarves, but he was half-orcen and had a glint of evil in his yellow eyes.

The Risker leaned forward. "The chase is over! Surrender or die!"

Grey Cloak stood with Dyphestive. "So what do you want to do?"

"We have to protect the dwarves. Not one of them can die. We need them."

Rhonna butted in. "We can take care of ourselves." She winked at them. "Whatever you decide to do, we're with you."

"I'm Grey Cloak. Perhaps you've heard of me," he said to the Risker.

"Can't say that I have, but I'm Commander Azzark. Perhaps you've heard of me."

"No, I can't say that I have either. How disappointing. As for surrender, well, we can't do that."

Commander Azzark gave a raspy chuckle then grabbed his bow. "Well, Grey Cloak, prepare to die with all your friends."

Dyphestive cocked the Iron Sword over his shoulder and said, "There won't be any holding back today."

"No, not this time," Grey Cloak agreed.

The dwarves popped the corks off their potions. Some of them drank, but others didn't.

Rhonna chugged down part of hers and handed the rest over to another. "This is it, dwarves! A bloody fight to the bitter end."

Commander Azzark fired the first shot from his bow. The bright head of the wizard-fire-charged arrow careened toward Rhonna.

Zanna deflected it with a small buckler of her own energy. "He's a natural. Be wary." She pulled both of her blades. "But I will handle him!" She sped toward Commander Azzark at an inhuman pace.

"Good idea," Grey Cloak said. He flipped the Rod of Weapons end over end and fired energy into the middling dragon and rider nearest him. The barbed bolts of energy lodged in the dragon's neck and exploded.

The middling shrieked and bucked, tossing the rider. His head tilted from where the neck was split open, and he blindly charged into another dragon as a fountain of fire spit out of the wound.

"That was nasty," Dyphestive said as he advanced. "I'll have to see what I can do to top that." He advanced toward a dragon bearing down on him. The dragon sucked in his breath to unleash a wave of fire. Dyphestive swung the Iron Sword, and the blade bit into the dragon's head as flames spit out.

The gem mounted in the sword's cross guard flared. Energy shot through Dyphestive's body. A burst of mystic fire spread from the blade and into the dragon, and his scales started to smoke. Then the beast exploded. *Boomph!*

Dyphestive held up his sword, gaping.

"What did you do?" Grey Cloak asked.

"I don't know. But it felt good!" He turned his gaze on the wide-eyed warrior who had fallen off the dragon and was standing in ashes up to his knees.

The Risker drew his sword and charged. He tried to feint left and stab right, but Dyphestive adjusted his swing, and in a stroke as fast as lightning, he cut the man through the torso. Another pulse of energy fired from the sword, and the Risker eroded into ash.

"Whoa!" Dyphestive said.

"I think you have their attention, brother," Grey Cloak said of the wary-eyed enemies. "Whatever you're doing, I say keep doing it!"

Dyphestive's blood caught fire. He bellowed a war cry and charged.

A Risker turned his dragon away and fired an arrow at Dyphestive. The missile whizzed into Dyphestive's shoulder, tearing through muscle and skin. But he didn't slow.

The dragon struck at Dyphestive with a flick of his tail, but he tried to hop over it. The tail smacked his heels and flipped him flat onto his back. He looked up in time to see the tail coming down on him like a hammer. When he swung, metal clipped scale, and scale turned to ash. *Poof!*

"I'll be," Dyphestive said as he rose to one knee. He spotted the Risker fumbling through the ash with a bewildered expression. "Never look a gift horse in the mouth." He charged.

The Risker ran, but Dyphestive caught up with him in three great strides. He poked the man in the back with the tip of his sword, and the Risker burst like a bubble made of ash.

"It shouldn't be so easy." He looked at his sword. "But I'm not complaining."

He scanned the area for his newest foe. The Riskers were moving away from him and attacking the others. One of the dragons sped toward Rhonna and the dwarves. They didn't see it coming.

"Rhonna! Watch out!"

The warning came too late. Dragon jaws closed around Rhonna's body.

"Rhonna!"

Zanna had fought numerous enemies over the decades, but she despised none more than the Riskers. They were traitors to the Sky Riders and turned dragons into abominations. On the Day of Betrayal, they'd turned the world of Gapoli upside down. Once guardians of all life, they became perversions of good and chose the side of evil.

That evil ran deep in Commander Azzark's veins. Arrogant confidence lurked in the man's eyes. He had no compassion and was only a cold and calculating servant of destruction. And his day of reckoning had come.

The grand dragon breathed out a smothering blanket of fire, blocking Zanna's charge. Her fleet feet propelled her into an inhuman hurdle, and she sailed above the fire, landed on the dragon's great head, and held on to one of his big horns with one hand.

"Hello, Commander Azzark. Allow me to introduce myself. Zanna Paydark."

His eyebrows rose. "I thought you were dead."

"You've been misinformed. I'm quite alive and very angry about my lengthy catatonic state." Her sword brightened. "And I think I'm going to take it out on you and your dragon."

45

THE MIDDLING DRAGON'S teeth pressed down on Rhonna's hips. The pressure built up like she was being squeezed in a vise, though he seemed to be unable to crush her.

She looked the dragon in the eyes and laughed. "What's the matter, you oversize lizard? Am I too tough for you to chew?" She held a hammer used for repairs on Crane's wagon and used it to strike the dragon in the eye. "How's that feel?"

The dragon reared and shook her, twisting his head from side to side like a dog killing its prey.

"Easy! You're making me sick! I guess that potion doesn't work on everything." She'd taken the potion of steel skin, and the dragon's teeth hadn't left a mark. She cracked him in the eye again with her hammer. "Take that! And that!"

The beast's jaws opened, and he spit her out.

Rhonna bounced once and rolled across the ground. When she came up to her knees, she found the dragon looming over her and sucking in his breath. "I don't know that I'm fireproof, though." She started to dive, but her feet slipped.

One of the four dwarves chucked a potion vial into the dragon's mouth, and he gulped it down.

The fire building in his mouth died, and his fiendish eyes widened as he shrank down to no bigger than a large dog, with the Risker still straddling it.

As the dragon shrank, a black-bearded dwarf grew to the height of a giant. He looked down on the dragon and his rider, lifted his horse-sized boot, and stomped the enemy into the ground. Bone and metal crunched and cracked.

The dwarf twisted his boot back and forth, pulverizing the Risker down to nothing.

"Huzzah!" Rhonna said.

Another dwarf, rotund with a fluffy chestnut beard, joined her and handed her a short sword. He gave her a nod and a grunt then took off with a dagger in each hand.

"Whoa, I've never seen a dwarf move so fast," she said.

The brown-bearded dwarf jumped away from a striking dragon's tail then ran up the back of the beast and plowed into a Risker aiming an arrow at him. Before the Risker could draw back the string, two daggers had been punched into his chest.

"Huzzah!" the triumphant dwarf screamed. He pulled his daggers from the man's chest and began hacking into the dragon's wings.

The dragon turned his head around and spewed fire. Flames covered the dwarf.

Rhonna's heart sank.

When the fiery breath cleared, the dwarf was gone. She looked to her side, and the dwarf was standing beside her with a smile.

She shook her head. "Don't do that again. It made my spine tingle."

Zanna pierced the hard skull of the dragon all the way down to the gray matter and sent a charge of wizard fire through her sword. Flames shot out of the dragon's earholes, and he sank to the ground.

"No!" an aghast Commander Azzark shouted. "I've been with Hvel since I was a child."

"Don't worry. You'll be joining him soon enough." Zanna jumped at the Risker.

Azzark created a mystic shield and absorbed her strike. "I will avenge my dragon, dead or alive! Look around you! Up in the skies! Your tricks won't outlast our numbers!"

"A shame you won't be around to see how it turns out!" She pulled her sword free of the shield and attacked again with both weapons. The shield caught them and held them fast, so she pushed harder. Her blades began to inch forward, bearing down on the man's chest.

Commander Azzark rotated his shield, forcing her wrists to twist. "I know every trick, Zanna. Believe me when I say that I'll be around long enough to see you die. To see all of you die."

She ripped her swords out of his shield, did a backflip off the dragon, and stood facing him. "Come on down from your dead pet and join me for a dance, Azzark. I challenge you, rider to rider."

"What sort of challenge are you offering? Me against you? You win and walk away? I win, and you surrender?" He sneered. "What sort of fool would take that bet when our victory is certain?" He waved his arm.

A middling dive-bombed Zanna.

She took cover under the dead dragon's wing. Talons skimmed her head as it shot by.

When she popped out of her position, Commander Azzark was gone. He'd hitched a ride on another grand dragon.

She shook her fist at him. "Coward!"

Grey Cloak stood in the inferno of dragon flame and waited. The Cloak of Legends insulated him like a warm winter blanket. Sweat beaded on his forehead, but that was the extent of the damage.

The dragon had a blank look on his face, and the Risker stood in his saddle and gaped.

Grey Cloak smirked. "Surprise." The head of the Rod of Weapons flamed up, and he jabbed and pierced the dragon's skull.

An arrow sped into his path, but he dodged it, stepping on the dragon's skull between the horns and vaulting himself at the Risker.

The Risker tried to parry with his bow, but Grey Cloak hit the man square in the face and knocked his helmet off. Then he snaked a dagger out of his belt and stabbed the enemy's shoulder.

The Risker roared, "Gar!"

With a windmill flip of the Rod of Weapons, Grey Cloak pierced the man's heart.

The ground had become a battlefield of dead dragons and men. The charred ground smoked, and the first wave of the enemy had been defeated.

A giant black-bearded dwarf stood out the most. Dragon blood dripped from his hands and beard. Another dwarf zipped around like a hummingbird. Rhonna stood near the wagon with Shannon, Crane, and two other dwarves.

Dyphestive and Zanna approached, looking into the sky. Fourteen more dragon riders circled above, waiting.

"I don't suppose your sword was big enough to scare them all off," Grey Cloak said.

"Afraid not."

Zanna put away her sword. "Commander Azzark is no fool. He can tell our resources are limited. What do you want to do?"

Grey Cloak shrugged. "I have no idea."

46

RISKERS CIRCLED IN THE SKY. Fourteen riders and dragons were more than a match for the small remnant of Talon, whose resources were becoming depleted. The giant black-bearded dwarf had started to shrink, and the speed of the dwarf with a fuzzy brown beard was gone.

Grey Cloak checked his inner pockets and pulled out one more potion. He recognized the strange lettering—vitality. It was more or less a healing potion, of which they had a few.

Zanna joined him with a vial in her hand. She flipped it end over end. "This is dragon breath. It's all I have left."

He swung his gaze over to Crane, who sat in the shade of the wagon, dripping with sweat. "Any tricks in your bag?"

Crane dabbed his face with a silk cloth. "I'm afraid not."

He glanced upward. "I think they're waiting for us to cook alive."

"They can cook us whenever they want," Grey Cloak said. "There's enough fire in those lizard lungs to lay waste to an entire city. We need to get to the hills and buy time."

Leaning on his sword, Dyphestive said, "I suggest we divide our forces and divide theirs at the same time."

"I thought about that. But I fear they'd gang up on the inferior group and come back for the rest. No, we need to stick together. It's our only chance." Gazing above, Grey Cloak asked, "What are they waiting for?"

"They're patient predators," Rhonna said. She tapped her hammer against her palm. "But they won't wait for long. You know that. They'll rain down fire from the heavens. I've seen them do that and burn my dwarves alive."

Crane said, "Perhaps we should surrender."

Everyone gave him disappointed looks.

"What?" Crane asked with a shrug. "Wave the white flag and buy more time. We don't have to really surrender, only make them think we are. It's not an awful idea."

"No, it isn't. But we need to make them think we're ready to fight." Grey Cloak pointed at the dragons. "Make them think we have something in store for them—an ultimate weapon, perhaps."

"I think Azzark is wary. He knows there are more naturals down here, but he doesn't know how many." Zanna extended her hand. "Let me see the Rod of Weapons."

He tossed it to her.

She ran her fingers over the beaten lacquered black surface and said, "Perhaps we do have an ultimate weapon, and we can send a message."

"What do you have in mind?" Grey Cloak asked.

"If we summon our wizard fire together and channel it through the rod, we'll give them a scare they'll never forget."

Grey Cloak smirked. "I like it." He turned and approached the toppled wagon. "Sorry about the stallion, Crane. But we're going to need to free your wagon."

Crane pushed himself up to his feet with a grunt. "It was his time. He was happy to die in a blaze of glory. So, what's your plan?"

"Zanna, do we have any potions of haste left?"

The brown-bearded dwarf tossed Grey Cloak his vial. "I left a few swallows."

"Thank you." Grey Cloak took the vial and handed it to Dyphestive. "Hang on to this."

"Why?"

"Because you're going to pull us to safety in those hills. But first..." He joined Zanna. "Let's send Commander Azzark a memorable message."

"Agreed." Zanna held out the Rod of Weapons, and Grey Cloak took hold. She gazed at the dragons circling in the sky. "Pick one."

"How about the one with the fiery-orange scales? He's a big one."

"And the bigger they are, the harder they fall." Zanna's eyes shone like hot steel. "Let's take them down, son."

Grey Cloak's wizard fire swelled inside him and spread into the rod. His energy merged with hers, and they became one. The exhilarating sensation was like fuel tossed onto a bonfire. He set his eyes on the target dragon and asked, "Ready?"

"Ready!"

The tip of the Rod of Weapons blossomed like a flower, and a bolt of bright-blue energy shot into the sky. It tore through the grand dragon's chest of armored scales and pushed the rider from her saddle.

The dragon roared, pounding his wings in desperation. The rider fell to the earth with the sound of metal crunching on stone. She started to stand and looked up in time to watch her dragon land on top of her.

"Huzzah!" the dwarves cried as they pumped their meaty fists in the air.

"That was beautiful!" Rhonna said.

Grey Cloak and Zanna set down the rod.

His hands burned, and he labored to catch his breath. "That was impressive!"

"Indeed," she said from one knee. Her hands were smoking. "And painful."

"Are you well?"

"I'll make it."

The Riskers flew to a higher elevation.

Grey Cloak turned his attention to Rhonna and Dyph-estive. "I think we scared the chipmunks out of them. Get that wagon ready. We need to rest."

47

THE DWARVES REMOVED Charger from the mangled harness.

Dyphestive pushed the wagon back over on its wheels and let the dwarves hitch him back up. "This again, huh?"

"I can't think of any better ideas," Grey Cloak said. He waved his arm. "Everyone, into the wagon. It's time to roll." He patted his brother on the chest. "You can handle this, can't you?"

Dyphestive shifted his brawny shoulders in his harness, and with a determined glare at the hills ahead, he said, "There's nothing I'd rather do."

"Good. That's what I like to hear. Now, drink up. Every last drop."

The ceramic vial appeared too small for Dyphestive's oversize hands. He flipped the cork off with his thumb and drank. His lips twitched, and he swallowed again. A moment later, he said, "Want to race?"

"You're dreaming if you think you can outrun me, potion or not."

Dyphestive clawed the ground with his boot and snorted like a wild horse. "Get in. I'm ready to run."

Crane took his customary seat on the bench, lifted his horse whip, and thought the better of it. He handed the lash to Shannon, who sat beside him. "Probably not a good idea."

"Nope."

The wagon started to roll.

Grey Cloak jumped into the bed, joining the dwarves and Zanna. "To the hills!"

Zanna kept the Rod of Weapons pointed at the sky. "They'll come, but we can't blast them all out of the sky. We don't have the strength between us."

"No, but we can make a shield to deflect their fire," he suggested.

They picked up speed.

Grey Cloak stood up behind Crane and Shannon and placed his hands on their shoulders. The wind rustled their hair, making it fly behind them.

Dyphestive trucked over the road, getting faster with every step.

The air whistled.

"Ha ha!" Grey Cloak said. "He's doing it! I would never

have imagined he could run so fast, with or without magic!"

"That's fast, all right!" Crane said. "He's running like a horse. Faster, even!"

"Grey!" Zanna shouted. "They're coming!"

The flying dragons' circle broke off smoothly into a V formation, and they dove toward the wagon.

He moved beside his mother and grabbed the staff. "I've never used this for a shield."

"It will work," she said. "You channel the energy. I'll shape it, like Tatiana's Star of Light."

Grey Cloak nodded. Still weary from using his energy earlier, he reached deep and brought the wizard fire forth.

A plume of light grew on the Rod of Weapons then spread over the wagon like a cloud.

A pair of middling dragons broke free of the flight pattern and dove toward the wagon. They raced overhead and breathed down fire.

Flames spread over the shield's surface and heated the air. It roared like fires in a great oven.

"It's working!" Zanna said, her face perspiring. "Hold on!"

Repelling the dragons' breath sucked more energy out of Grey Cloak. "I am!"

The flames died. The dragons broke off their attack and rose back into the sky.

"Should we let the shield down and rest?" Zanna asked.

The Riskers fired arrows as they turned away. The mystically charged bolts ricocheted off the shield.

"No, too dangerous." He turned to the front. They were closing in on the hills in the east, but it would take some time. "I can hold it. I have to!"

Two more dragons dropped away from the formation. They flew alongside the wagon, unleashing their breath.

"Great gophers!" Rhonna said. "It's getting as hot as a furnace in here."

The dragons came on, wave after wave, hitting the shield with flaming breath and sucking away more energy.

The Rod of Weapons turned hot.

Zanna's brow furrowed, and she shared concerned looks with Grey Cloak.

"Dyphestive, run faster!" he yelled.

"I don't think he can. He's giving it all he has," Crane said.

The wagon thundered down the plains, leaving a cloud of dust behind it.

"We're getting close," Shannon said.

Eight dragons jetted ahead of the others and streaked over the wagon.

"It looks like they're going to wall us off from the rocks," Rhonna said. "I don't suppose your brother can plow through them."

Grey Cloak shook his head. "Once we stop, run for the hills, everyone. We'll hold the Riskers off the best we can."

The mesh-like shield started to crack against the flames. Sections began to flake off and dissipate.

The fire-breathing dragons veered away, and the Riskers fired another volley. A glowing arrow snuck through the gap in the shield, burying itself in Rhonna's shoulder blade.

"Gar! What sort of coward shoots a dwarf in the back!" She stretched her arm over her shoulder, reaching for the shaft. "Get it out!"

The blond-bearded dwarf grabbed the arrow, looked Rhonna in the eye, and yanked it out.

"Gar! That hurts!"

"Grey Cloak!" Shannon shouted. She pointed ahead.

He moved toward the front.

A wall of Riskers stood between them and the hills.

"Dyphestive! What do you want to do?" he shouted.

With a snarl, Dyphestive said, "Give me my sword! I'm going through!"

48

Dyphestive bull-rushed the dragon breathing at him like a juggernaut on fire. He plowed through the flames and plunged hot steel into the chest of the beast.

Unlike last time, there was no *poof* sound, no ashes, and no disintegration—only the agonizing howl of the dragon, who roared his last breath at the top of his lungs.

"Aaargh!" he bellowed. "It's thunder time!" He pulled his sword free and found Lythlenion by his side, yanking him out of the harness.

"That's my line," Lythlenion said with a fierce orcen grin.

"Sorry, but I like it."

"You do it great honor." Lythlenion ripped him free of the last straps. "Bloody biscuits, those dwarves made the straps tight. What I would do to have Thunderash in my grip once more. But I'm not entirely useless. Everyone, close your eyes and grab something heavy." His eyes turned as white as ice, and he pressed his hands together. "A storm is coming."

"You can say that again." Dyphestive freed the Iron Sword and set his eyes on the Risker closest to him. "You're going to die!"

Before the warrior drew his sword, Dyphestive hurled the Iron Sword like a javelin into the man's chest.

The Risker gawped and clutched at the great blade then fell off the back of his dragon.

All of a sudden, a strong wind picked up. Dust devils popped up all over and moved toward the middling dragons.

Riskers were ripped out of their saddles and flipped head over heels. The force of the wind carried them higher and higher. A dragon opened his wings and was carried backward into another.

Everyone clung to the wagon and one another as the powerful wind pulled at their clothing and feet.

"Dyphestive!" Lythlenion shouted. "Great is your weight. Use it to your advantage while my abilities hold!"

"Not a problem!" Still quickened by the potion, he took his sword from the dead Risker's body and sped into another attack.

A dragon blew fire at him only to have it blow back in his face.

Dyphestive split open the dragon's head right between the horns with the edge of his sword.

One of the beasts crept behind him and took a swipe at his back, opening a nasty gash.

"Augh!" With an angry growl, he turned and severed the dragon's neck.

Dyphestive spotted another dragon lurking near Lythlenion, crouched low and ready to spring. "Watch out!"

Eyes narrowed, the great lizard scurried beneath the wind, jaws wide, and pounced at Lythlenion.

Dyphestive sped across the short distance then leaped and hit the dragon a split second before the dragon bit Lythlenion's leg. He freed his grip on the Iron Sword and locked his arms around the beast's tremendous neck. "Let go!"

Suddenly, Lythlenion's spell faded, and Riskers rained down from the sky. Dust was everywhere, covering men, beasts, and wagon.

Dyphestive's Herculean muscles bulged. "Hurk!" He squeezed the monster's neck with all his might. Scale and sinew started to pop. "Let go of my friend!" He opened his mouth and bit the dragon in the neck, tearing off scales and flesh. "Now!"

The dragon's jaws slackened, and Lythlenion kicked free and crawled backward.

Huffing and puffing, Dyphestive applied more pressure. Finally, the dragon's neck snapped. Gasping for breath, he let the monster slide out of his trembling arms. "How are you?"

"The bite is deep, but I can mend it," the orcen priest-warrior said. "Thank you, brother."

"You're welcome."

The moment the stormy wind started to die, Grey Cloak led the company into the rocky hills.

Dyphestive brought up the rear, carrying Lythlenion over his shoulder.

All of them made it to the rocky sanctuary then kept moving higher, looking for a spot to hide.

Half of Commander Azzark's troops were still on the ground, including him. They were counting their dead.

"Well, we've given him plenty to think about before he attacks again," Grey Cloak said as he jumped from one rock to another. "Keep moving. We should be able to rest soon."

"I don't think we're out of danger." Zanna pointed at the sky. "Look."

A team of Riskers soared overhead and formed a tight circle right above them.

"Dragon eyes are keener than an eagle's. They won't be losing track of us anytime soon," Zanna added.

"True, but they won't be able to attack us in bunches either. The rocks will give us cover," Grey Cloak replied. But he knew they were trapped like a ship in a bottle. All the enemy needed to do was wait them out—or flush them out with flame.

We've bought all the time we're going to buy. I need to find a way to finish this.

Grey Cloak reached into his pockets and grabbed the Figurine of Heroes.

"What are you planning to do with that?" Zanna asked.

Eyeing the artifact, he said, "I think it might make a fine present for Commander Azzark. Perhaps it will ruin his day and scare the others away."

"Well, it's still a long walk to the sanctuary. And we still need the Stone of Transport," Zanna said.

"I know. I can't believe Chopper put us in this bind. If we don't get the stone back, Black Frost might as well have won."

"One battle at a time," Dyphestive said. He set Lythlenion down in the shade, and the orc started working on his leg.

Grey Cloak handed a vial of healing to his brother. "Give him this."

Down on the dusty plains, Commander Azzark's forces regrouped. Not all of the Riskers who'd fallen from the sky were dead. It appeared two dragons and riders had survived the fight and were ready to battle on. They marched forward and entered the base of the hills then began to climb.

"Fantastic," Crane said from his spot behind the rocks. "Those dragons won't have any trouble sniffing us out. There's no place to hide." He counted on his stubby fingers. "There's too many of them. Too blooming many!"

49

***

CRANE WAS RIGHT, and Grey Cloak wished he couldn't have been more wrong. The dragons would have no trouble tracking them. He looked at his brother and shrugged. "No choice now. We can only take down as many as we can take down. Let's find good ground." On weary limbs, he made his way up the rocks. "It's time to fight another fight."

"I'm with you, brother." Dyphestive made his way up to Grey Cloak with the Iron Sword resting on his shoulder. "We've come far. You've done great. I want you to know I'm proud of you. Proud to be your brother."

"And I, you."

Zanna met up with them and said, "I'll do what I can to shield us from the forces in the sky. Using these rocks, I can harness my wizardry to make barriers." Her hand trembled when she brushed her hair from her eyes. "I'm proud of both of you boys."

Grey Cloak nodded and pointed at a spot higher in the rocks, where the boulders formed a channel. "We can fight from there. But we have to be careful that we don't get cooked inside. Up, everyone. Up. We can't let them catch up to us."

Rhonna, the dwarves, Lythlenion, Shannon, and Crane traversed the rough terrain, up the slope and into the gap.

Dyphestive guarded the entrance with Grey Cloak.

As Zanna made her way into the gap, energy spread through her fingertips and created a ceiling that joined the narrow channel together.

"What do you say, brother?" Grey Cloak asked as he tossed the Figurine of Heroes up and down. "How about one last surprise?"

Dyphestive nodded. "Go for it. After all, I've never tried to stop you before."

"Ha! You haven't, have you?"

"No. But then again, I can be a donkey skull."

"I know better than that." Grey Cloak cocked back his arm and hurled the figurine. It tumbled through the air in a high arc and descended toward the wave of dragons crawling up the hills. It bounced on one rock and landed upright on another.

The Riskers spotted the object and slowed.

Dyphestive nodded at his brother.

Grey Cloak took a breath and said, *"Osid-ayan-umra-shokrah-ha!"*

Inky-black smoke shot out of the figurine's head and covered the rocks, moving like fog in all directions.

"I can't see a thing," Dyphestive said. He fanned the smoke from his face. "That's as thick as soup."

Rhonna called, "What's that? What did you do? Did you use that stupid figurine again? I can't see a wart on an ogre's nose in this."

Grey Cloak's skin prickled. He turned on the flame of the Rod of Weapons as an eerie silence fell over the hills. "Be ready. Sometimes this doesn't go so well."

With both hands on the handle of his sword, Dyphestive said, "You don't have to tell me."

The breeze started to carry the smoke away from the hills.

A winged humanoid figure stood on the rocks, looking down on the blood brothers with his arms crossed over his chest. He had a dragon-like face, two horns, and a body wrapped in tiny serpentine scales that shone like silver. It was a dragon who stood like a man.

Grey Cloak had never seen the likes of such a dragon nor one so majestic. He met its glaring blue eyes and said, "Hello."

In a mannerly voice as polished as the silver that coated his body, the dragon said, "I take it you're the one who summoned me from my world. I am Slivver, at your service.

Might I ask why you've ripped me from my world and into this one?"

Dyphestive pointed at the enemies on the land and in the sky. "We need a hand battling them."

Slivver probed the airways. "Sluggish brutes, aren't they? Ugly too." He bent down and sniffed Grey Cloak and Dyphestive. "I smell my brother on you."

"Of what brother do you speak?"

"His name is Nath."

They shared shocked looks.

"You're Nath's brother?" Grey Cloak asked.

"Favorite brother," Slivver stated. "I've been searching for him. Where is he?"

"He's in Safe Haven," Grey Cloak said excitedly. "We're in this fight to save him and this world!"

"And those brutes stand in the way." Slivver locked his taloned fingers together, flexed them, and cracked them. "Let me see what I can do." He stretched out his wings. "Be certain to tell my brother hello, in case I don't get a chance to see him. Tell him I miss him. We all dearly do."

"We will!" Dyphestive said.

Slivver streaked down the hill like a silver sparrow. A volley of Riskers' arrows skipped off his skin.

The silver dragon turned toward the nearest middling dragon and rider and scorched them both with a mouthful of blue flames. He jumped and flipped end over end then jetted toward the ring of dragons circling above Talon.

"Zooks! That's the fastest dragon I've ever seen!" Grey Cloak said. "Watch him go!"

Slivver grabbed a Risker by the collar, yanked him from the saddle, and dropped him. Before the man had landed, Slivver grabbed another enemy and flung him across the sky.

"Whoa!" Dyphestive said. "That *is* fast!"

The flying dragons changed direction, spreading out, and tried to get their bearings on Slivver as he moved like a fly in the sky. They shot arrow after arrow at the frighteningly fast enemy.

Slivver dodged the glowing missiles with feline agility. He sank his bottom talons into a Risker's shoulders and breathed fire, turning the rider into flames.

Grey Cloak tore his gaze away from Slivver. Below, Commander Azzark had resumed the climb up the hills at a quickened pace.

Slapping his gawking brother on the back, Grey Cloak said, "They're coming!"

Dyphestive nodded and brought his sword to bear. "I'm ready."

Above, Slivver was creating havoc among the Riskers. He shot up to the sky and hung in the air, tilting his head over one shoulder then the other. He pointed east and shrugged.

The flying middling dragons pounced toward the stranger from another world.

Slivver's glistening scales started to dull, and his body began to dissipate.

The enemies flew straight through the cloud of Slivver.

Grey Cloak's stomach sank into his toes. As quickly as Slivver had come, he began to vanish. "He's gone!"

"Oh my," Dyphestive replied. "That was fast. You did your best." He faced Commander Azzark's troops. "It's all on us now."

Grey Cloak stood shoulder to shoulder with his brother and said, "It's thunder time!"

Dyphestive laughed like a wild man and charged down the hill.

50

As his brother charged down the rocks, Grey Cloak caught a glimpse of the dragon riders in the sky. The dragons pivoted in a tight circle and headed west. The lead Riskers of the V formation signaled to Commander Azzark's forces on the ground.

What's going on now? What was Slivver pointing at earlier?

He turned his upward gaze east. *Oh no!*

Another group of dragons was flying toward them.

"Zanna! We're going to have more company!" he shouted. "Dyphestive! Get back here!"

His brother skidded to a stop and stood on one of the boulders.

Grey Cloak pointed at the sky. "Get back here! We have to take cover!" He waved Dyphestive back. "Hurry, brother. Hurry!"

Sword in hand, Dyphestive stood on the rock and shook his head. "I'm not going anywhere."

Commander Azzark's ground forces stopped their advance, searching the skies with puzzled expressions.

Grey Cloak turned his attention to the new wave of dragons closing in on them at an alarming speed. The lead dragon was a huge grand. Sunlight reflected off the splashes of gold on his scales. On his back rode a warrior in bright, shining armor. Sun-bleached hair spilled from under the helmet.

The grand dragon roared with the voice of a dozen thunderstorms.

Grey Cloak's heart leaped as the dragons raced overhead. He let out a wild cheer. "It's Cinder! Look! It's Anya and Cinder!"

Behind Cinder, eight more dragons and their riders chased the Riskers across the sky.

Grey Cloak couldn't believe his eyes. He spotted Zora, Gorva, and Razor, who were armed to the teeth with full dragon armor and riding like the wind.

A familiar dragon peeled away, dragging his twin tails behind him.

"Streak!" Grey Cloak screamed. "My brother!"

Streak pulled up and made a soft landing on the rocks beside him.

"How'd you get here so fast?" Grey Cloak asked.

"We started flying the moment that hairy nugget of a

gnome stole the Stone of Transport from you," Streak said. "We watched the entire event from the Eye of the Sky Riders. Been flying ever since with a little help from enchanted harnesses." He puffed his chest out, revealing the well-crafted leather harness buckled to it. "I thought it would slow me down, but these made us stronger and faster. Otherwise, the big ones would never have kept up."

A shadow passed overhead.

Rock, a muscular grand with dark-blue scales that were almost black, landed near Dyphestive. His horns were massive, like his father's, and smoke streamed from his nose. He said in a very deep voice to Dyphestive, "What are you waiting for, Thin Skin?" He lowered his body. "We came here to battle, not to stand around."

A big-eyed Dyphestive didn't hesitate to climb into the saddle. "It's good to see you, Rock!" He nodded at Grey Cloak. "We're going down that hill. Care to join us?"

Grey Cloak shook his head as he climbed onto Streak's back. "How about this: you hit them low, and we'll hit them high."

Dyphestive grabbed his dragon's reins. "Thunderbolts! I like it!"

Rock lifted his head, reared, and breathed a geyser of flames. His feet came down with a thud, crushing boulders. He faced the enemy, roared like a thousand lions, lowered his horns, and said, "It's thunder time!"

"Up, Streak!" Grey Cloak said with a hungry-for-battle

grin. The arrival of his friends had renewed him from limb to limb. "Ride the sky, brother! Ride the sky!"

Will Talon and the sons and daughters of Cinder triumph over superior forces?

Can Tiny locate Chopper and return the Stone of Transport in time?

What about Black Frost? How can he be slowed if he cannot be stopped?

With only one book left, prepare yourself for one of the greatest fantasy battles royal of all time! Grab a copy of Dark Mountain: Dragon Wars #20, on sale now! LINK!

AND PLEASE LEAVE A REVIEW FOR THUNDER TIME! THANKS SO MUCH! LINK!

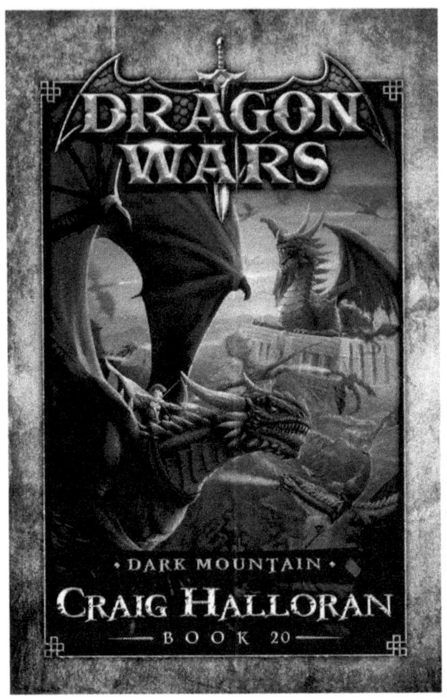

And if you haven't already, signup for my newsletter and grab 3 FREE books including the Dragon Wars Prequel.
WWW.DRAGONWARSBOOKS.COM

Teachers and Students, if you would like to order paperback copies for you library or classroom, email craig@thedarkslayer.com to receive a special discount.

Gear up in this Dragon Wars body armor enchanted with a +2 Coolness factor/+4 at Gaming Conventions. Sizes range from halfling (Small) to Ogre (XXL). LINK . www.society6.com

ABOUT THE AUTHOR

*Check me out on Bookbub and follow: HalloranOn-BookBub

*I'd love it if you would subscribe to my mailing list: www.craighalloran.com

*On Facebook, you can find me at The Darkslayer Report or Craig Halloran.

*Twitter, Twitter, Twitter. I am there, too: www.twitter.com/CraigHalloran

*And of course, you can always email me at craig@thedarkslayer.com

See my book lists below!

OTHER BOOKS

Craig Halloran resides with his family outside his home-town of Charleston, West Virginia. When he isn't entertaining mankind, he is seeking adventure, working out, or watching sports. To learn more about him, go to www.thedarkslayer.com.

Check out all my great stories...

Free Books

    The Red Citadel and the Sorcerer's Power

    The Darkslayer: Brutal Beginnings

    Nath Dragon—Quest for the Thunderstone

The Chronicles of Dragon Series 1 (10-book series)

    The Hero, the Sword and the Dragons (Book 1)

Dragon Bones and Tombstones (Book 2)

Terror at the Temple (Book 3)

Clutch of the Cleric (Book 4)

Hunt for the Hero (Book 5)

Siege at the Settlements (Book 6)

Strife in the Sky (Book 7)

Fight and the Fury (Book 8)

War in the Winds (Book 9)

Finale (Book 10)

Boxset 1-5

Boxset 6-10

Collector's Edition 1-10

Tail of the Dragon, The Chronicles of Dragon, Series 2 (10-book series)

Tail of the Dragon #1

Claws of the Dragon #2

Battle of the Dragon #3

Eyes of the Dragon #4

Flight of the Dragon #5

Trial of the Dragon #6

Judgement of the Dragon #7

Wrath of the Dragon #8

Power of the Dragon #9

Hour of the Dragon #10

Boxset 1-5

Boxset 6-10

Collector's Edition 1-10

The Odyssey of Nath Dragon Series (New Series) (Prequel to Chronicles of Dragon)

Exiled

Enslaved

Deadly

Hunted

Strife

The Darkslayer Series 1 (6-book series)

Wrath of the Royals (Book 1)

Blades in the Night (Book 2)

Underling Revenge (Book 3)

Danger and the Druid (Book 4)

Outrage in the Outlands (Book 5)

Chaos at the Castle (Book 6)

Boxset 1-3

Boxset 4-6

Omnibus 1-6

The Darkslayer: Bish and Bone, Series 2 (10-book series)

Bish and Bone (Book 1)

Black Blood (Book 2)

Red Death (Book 3)

Lethal Liaisons (Book 4)

Torment and Terror (Book 5)

Brigands and Badlands (Book 6)

War in the Wasteland (Book 7)

Slaughter in the Streets (Book 8)

Hunt of the Beast (Book 9)

The Battle for Bone (Book 10)

Boxset 1-5

Boxset 6-10

Bish and Bone Omnibus (Books 1-10)

CLASH OF HEROES: Nath Dragon meets The Darkslayer mini series

Book 1

Book 2

Book 3

The Henchmen Chronicles

The King's Henchmen

The King's Assassin

The King's Prisoner

The King's Conjurer

The King's Enemies

The King's Spies

The Gamma Earth Cycle

Escape from the Dominion

Flight from the Dominion

Prison of the Dominion

<u>The Supernatural Bounty Hunter Files (10-book series)</u>

Smoke Rising: Book 1

I Smell Smoke: Book 2

Where There's Smoke: Book 3

Smoke on the Water: Book 4

Smoke and Mirrors: Book 5

Up in Smoke: Book 6

Smoke Signals: Book 7

Holy Smoke: Book 8

Smoke Happens: Book 9

Smoke Out: Book 10

Boxset 1-5

Boxset 6-10

Collector's Edition 1-10

Zombie Impact Series

Zombie Day Care: Book 1

Zombie Rehab: Book 2

Zombie Warfare: Book 3

Boxset: Books 1-3

<u>OTHER WORKS & NOVELLAS</u>

The Red Citadel and the Sorcerer's Power

www.ingramcontent.com/pod-product-compliance
Lightning Source LLC
Chambersburg PA
CBHW070634310726
48982CB00001B/281